Other Books by Betty Baker

the
DUNDERHEAD
WAR

the DUNDERHEAD WAR

a novel by BETTY BAKER

HARPER & ROW, PUBLISHERS
New York, Evanston, and London

*To Jimmy, George, Theresa and Chris
who provided background noise
for the writing*

Contents

Map Illustrating the Mexican War

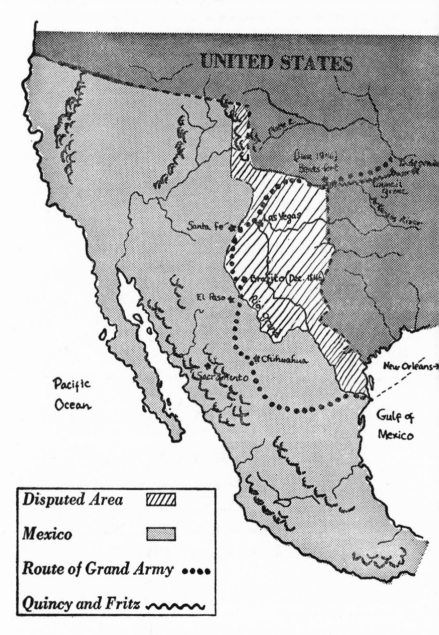

UNITED STATES

Pacific
Ocean

Santa Fe

Las Vegas

Bracito (Dec. 1846)

El Paso

Rio Grande

Chihuahua

Sacramento

New Orleans

Gulf of
Mexico

Disputed Area	//////
Mexico	
Route of Grand Army	••••
Quincy and Fritz	~~~~

1

An Almighty Itch

Biela's comet was over Missouri in mid-December, but we were two weeks into 1846 before a newspaper telling about it reached Pa's store in Independence. Pa studied the front page advertising while I read the rest of the paper out loud to Possible and the couple or three others who always lounged by our stove in winter. They had to jaw over everything I read, even the social doings of folks they didn't know and weren't likely to meet. I didn't get to read about the comet until after supper when Pa, Possible, and me were home in front of the kitchen fire.

"Comets are bad medicine," said Possible Gooch. "They're near as bad as blood on the moon."

Pa snorted. "That comet isn't going to end the world or set fire to the prairie."

"That's possible," admitted the old trapper, "seeing how it's so puny I can't make it out. But sure as God

1

raised humps on buffler, that comet's working up a spell of change and upheaval."

"Then I wish it would hurry and get on with it," I said.

A bit of upheaval wouldn't be unwelcome, but I mostly hoped for something to change Pa's mind about letting me travel to far places. I itched to see the things Possible told of, mountains with snow in summer, springs that boiled in winter, wild Indians, and the village the Russians had built on the California coast.

When Pa had gone to his room, I asked the trapper, "Can a comet affect people's reasoning?"

"It's possible. Anything like this sure stirs up the Injuns."

I waited till he'd rolled up in his blankets, feet to the fire, then took the candle into the lean-to where I slept. I lay there a long time, staring at the chinked boards and trying to figure a way to get shut of Independence. Thanks to Mama, I had more book learning than most folks and I could maybe run the store if Pa ever took sick. But I couldn't hunt, trap, trail, or do any of the things that counted on the prairie. Sure as sin I couldn't hire out to any emigrant train, and with Pa talking down every argument I thought up, my only hope seemed to be a far-off comet.

The winter wound out like all winters in Independence, about as lively as a Pawnee rattle without pebbles. The last wagon trains and fur trappers were long gone west. The Santa Fé traders that hadn't wintered in Mexico were downriver in St. Louis or New Orleans. The Indians holed up somewheres out on the

2

prairie and folks in Independence hunkered down by warm stoves and waited for spring.

It didn't matter which stove a body favored, the one with cast iron cupids in the Washington Hotel, the rusty pots in the taverns, or the log burner in Pa's store. The talk was the same, chawed-over politics, the future of Independence and whether mules or oxen made better teams. Far as I could see, the only change that winter of the comet was a new stoveside topic: war. Nobody doubted we'd fight one. The question was, who with?

Mexico still claimed Texas, though we'd made it the twenty-eighth state. Eastern papers had it that if the Mexicans declared war, France would fight alongside them to keep us from taking California. Some stove-siders laughed and said the Mexicans wouldn't fight, especially if Congress doctored their bruises with Yankee gold. That was always good for an afternoon's hoorah over why we should pay for Texas when it was already rightfully ours.

Like most folks, I thought we'd fight the British. They were dead set on keeping Oregon, though President Polk had sworn we'd hold onto the Oregon country clear to the 54° 40′ line. Some argued the President was fixing to settle for less, but anyone could see he was going to stand firm even if it meant war. Nobody worried. We'd whipped the Britishers twice. We could do it again. I just hoped the fighting wouldn't start for another year. When volunteers were called, I wanted to go.

Every snowfall Will Dayton and I met at the livery stable and drove the double-teamed snowplow down the McAdamized road to the river landing and the outlying

3

farms. There wasn't much snow that winter of the comet and I got so all-fired restless I started thinking I'd been wrong to quit my schooling when Mama died of the cholera. I went so far as to tromp the frozen road ruts to the schoolhouse and stand outside listening to the classes drone out their lessons. It made more sense than stoveside politics but I didn't go in. Even an under-growed seventeen feels foolish squeezing onto a school bench where the next oldest boy isn't over twelve.

Come March even Possible's tall tales of grizzlies, Indians, and Colter's Hell wore thin and wearisome. I kept dreaming over my favorite rifle, an old one with ivory buffalo heads set in the stock. Possible made up stories on why one of the buffalo heads had a broken horn while I planned a lifetime of scrapes and hard places that rifle would get me out of. I kept the head with the broken horn turned uppermost to discourage anyone from buying it. Not that there was any chance of my owning any rifle. Pa didn't hold with firearms except in the wilds, and the last year or two, Indepen-dence had gotten too civilized even for rabbit hunting.

Spring came earlier and wetter than any remem-bered in Missouri.

"It's that comet," said Possible.

I snorted like Pa. "Is that the most it can do?"

"Hold your fire, Quince. The stronger the medicine, the longer it takes to work."

But I'd given up on the comet. The spring thaw brought the mountain men from a winter of beaver trapping, raring to break loose and whoop it up. Every boat from St. Louis carried emigrants bound for

4

Oregon and California. They argued and dickered and caused near as much commotion as the trappers. Indians came to gawk and beg. The blacksmiths worked four forges day and night, hotels jammed three in a bed, and Pa sold barrels and cases fast as Possible and I could haul stock from the boat landing. Far as I could see, everything was disappointingly the same right down to the letter from Germany.

Far back as I could recollect, the spring mail had brought a letter from Uncle Fritz. Mama used to read each year's letter over and over. Fritz was a man growed, but to Mama he was always "little Fritz" or "my baby brother."

When I opened the letter, I said, "Looks like that comet didn't upheave Germany none either."

"Since when do you read German?" Pa asked.

Between Mama and the other Germans around Independence, Pa and me had learned to speak a little and understand more, but neither of us could cipher the funny script.

"The letter's shorter than ever. It figures things are downright dull over there too," I said.

"You can stop by Mueller's farm and ask him to read it." Pa handed me the bill of lading for the stock that had come upriver with the mail. "Dry goods. Better get out there before that calico's watersoaked."

"Where's Possible?"

"You'll have to load by yourself, Quincy. Fitzpatrick got in last night."

That meant Possible would be with the mountain man, whooping it up and sleeping it off, turn and turn about, until some trader sobered him for the trip to Santa Fé. Years of standing hip deep in icy streams setting beaver traps had given Possible joints that crippled in every chill. For three years the old man had worked as scout and hunter for Santa Fé traders in summer and wintered over with Pa. There wasn't a steadier man in Independence save when an old trapping crony hit town.

I grabbed my Mackinaw coat from the peg in the storeroom and left by the back door. The alley was no drier than the street but the mud wasn't churned as much. After the walk through misty drizzle, the livery stable felt warm and snug. I couldn't blame old Dolly for balking when I led her to the spring wagon. She knew it meant going out in the wet. Once outside, she lowered her head and plodded toward the river road, not turning aside for man nor chuckhole. She wanted only to reach the landing and get back in the warm, dry stable. I tried to swing around by the Independence House to ask Will what had the crowd there all stirred up, but Dolly's mouth was too hardened for rain or bit to have any effect. The bony old mare stopped when she pleased or when someone grabbed her halter and hung on.

"Hey, Quincy!" Will Dayton waved at me from the steps of his father's hotel. "Wait up, Quince."

"I'd sure like to," I called back. "But Dolly's not interested."

"She is now," said a hoarse voice. Dolly's head jerked sideways and she struggled to keep her footing in the slippery mud.

6

"Let her go, Rufus." I pulled the whip from its socket.

Rufus Purdy straightened and looked over Dolly's back. "You fixing to use that on me?"

That had been my intention but I thought better of it and put the whip away. None of the boys ever tangled with Rufus more than once, not if they could help it. I'd taken my beating five years back but I'd not forgotten.

"There's no need to throw her," I said.

"You wanted the nag stopped. I stopped her."

"Nobody asked you." Rufus wouldn't give his worst enemy a hard look without asking something in return. I didn't want him thinking he held a claim on me.

He came around Dolly, carrying something dark and lumpy under his tattered greatcoat. Will skidded up, spattering mud three yards in all directions. Rufus yelled and pulled his shabby coat tighter over the bundle.

"Sorry." But Will scarcely glanced at Rufus. "Are you going to the landing, Quince?"

"Sure, want to help me load?"

"Anything for a ride." Will glanced back at the Independence House. "Pa will have conniptions if I disappear now, but I heard a boat whistle awhile back. I just have to know if there's fresh news."

He grabbed hold to climb up. Rufus pushed him aside.

"I'm the one gets to ride to the landing," he said. "I didn't wrastle this stinking horse to accommodate you."

"Or me either," I pointed out. "Besides, Will asked first for the ride. Fair's fair."

Will grinned, but from the way Rufus scowled I knew there'd be an accounting made if I didn't offer something.

"You're welcome to ride in the back," I said. The wagon bed was harder than the road to redemption. I thought sure he'd turn it down but he nodded and started toward the rear of the wagon.

"Just a minute, Rufus." Will poked the bulge under Rufus's coat. "What are you hiding in there?"

"What's it to you?"

"Why, Quincy can't haul contraband. The Heffendorfs are respectable merchants. Honor is their cornerstone."

Rufus glanced up and I tried to look righteous.

"All right." His whispery voice sank even lower. "It's a buffalo robe I'm going to sell at the landing."

He pulled part of the mangy hide out to show us, then slopped back to the tailgate and climbed aboard. Will pulled himself up to the seat.

"Some poor Indian's going to wake up cold," he whispered.

Pa claimed there was nothing lower than men who sold whiskey to Indians unless it was the scum who robbed the Indians who drank it. Even careless emigrants were likely to wake up in the back alleys of Independence to find themselves stripped of all possessions. For years I'd heard talk about Rufus and his uncle, but I couldn't believe it of anyone I'd growed up with.

Rufus edged along the wagon bed and settled behind us. I flipped the reins and Dolly trudged forward.

"What's the big news at the Independence House?" I asked Will.

"General Taylor's in the Nueces Strip."

Mexico had finally given up on all of Texas and settled for claiming the Nueces River as the boundary, but Texas declared it was U.S. land all the way to the Rio Grande. General Taylor had been camped in Corpus Christi, inside the Nueces Strip, since January.

"Tell me something new," I asked.

"I did." Will's eyes sparkled. "Taylor's way inside the strip. He's blockading the Rio Grande."

I nearly dropped the reins. "The Mexicans will fight for sure!"

"Seems likely, but you haven't heard the biggest news. Fitzgerald met soldiers a couple or three days back. They told him President Polk is forming a Grand Army of the West from the Fort Leavenworth cavalry and Missouri volunteers. The governor's expected to call for enlistments any day."

"Grand Army, my stinking foot," Rufus rasped from behind us. "Forty dollars a year with nothing but moldy fatback on your stomach."

"I take it you're not overly anxious to join," Will said.

"I still got all my senses. I don't aim to get them blowed out."

I let Dolly pick her own way while I turned around to argue. "Do you want a foreign empire on American soil?"

"Don't make no never mind to me."

I rolled out all the things I'd read in the papers and

9

heard around the stove. About it being our destiny to spread from ocean to ocean and that if it was true the wilderness belonged to the people who settled it and tamed the Indians, then California and Oregon rightfully belonged to us. Americans already owned most of the land out there.

Rufus spat over the side of the wagon. "Let them join the army. I got no fight with Mexico."

I remembered something Pa and Possible often talked over. "What about that Texas force the Mexicans took prisoner a few years back? The ones they made draw beans."

One bean in every four had been black and meant death for the man who drew it. Not many of the Texicans had returned from that Mexican prison.

"What's that got to do with my volunteering?" asked Rufus.

"Didn't one of your kin draw a black bean?"

"That was his lookout."

"Don't you want to avenge him?" Will asked.

"If you mean am I going to join your Grand Stinking Army, no. Weak heads don't run in the Purdy family."

"Our country asks you to serve."

"Let the country serve me first, then I'll decide if it's worth it."

I jumped off the wagon, ran and caught Dolly's bridle. When the wagon stopped I walked back, climbed up beside Will, and stood facing Rufus. Anger shook me as if I had the ague.

"Get out," I told him.

"What for?"

"This is an American wagon. It doesn't haul traitors."

"It's a free country."

"Then I got a right to put you out."

"But it's more than a mile to the landing," Rufus complained.

"Get out!"

Will stood beside me, backing my play. Rufus studied us a minute. I wasn't tall and though Will could see over me, he was all bone. Even together we were no likely match for Rufus, but we were too mad to care. Rufus must've figured that gave us an edge. He climbed over the side of the wagon. Dolly started off on her own, jerking Will and me to the seat.

"I got a long memory, Quincy Heffendorf," he called after us. "You'll pay for every miserable stinking step from here to the landing."

Coming through the gray drizzle in that whispery voice of his, the promise sounded like something from a bad dream.

I shivered and asked Will, "How many steps do you figure?"

"If he breaks each finger and toe bone separate, you still don't have enough to go around."

"Still and all, I'm glad I did it."

"He's lucky it was us. If he'd talked like that in town, he'd have been carried out on a rail with a feather coat." Will put on the voice of the circuit preacher. "It was our bounden duty to show Brother Rufus the error

11

of his way. Brother Quince, you have saved him from a vile fate and taught him the perils of a wagging tongue."

But the words didn't lighten the weight in my stomach. The mist turned to real rain and I urged Dolly to a faster pace. I didn't relish being on the landing when Rufus dragged in. We jolted along, hunched against the rain and thinking about Rufus Purdy's threat of revenge.

Dolly halted on the landing and looked back as if asking me to get on with the loading. Rain never halted work when boats docked but more men stood around arguing than unloading. Everyone wanted their goods sooner than now, but nothing could move from the holds until some emigrant's broken-down wagon was repaired and hauled off the deck. Will discovered the last paddle wheeler upriver had brought written orders to open enlistments in the Missouri volunteers.

He thumped me on the back. "I'm joining no matter what Pa says. What about you, Quincy? Get yourself a horse and gun and we'll ride to Fort Leavenworth together."

"Sure thing. Just me and Dolly and Pa's old broken flintlock. Besides, I'm not eighteen till December."

"Sorry, Quince. I forgot."

"That's all right." But it wasn't. I wanted to join more than anything. It wasn't fair that someone like Rufus should be all of eighteen while I was seven months shy.

A deck hand told us the Heffendorf shipment wouldn't be out of the hold until tomorrow, which was fine by me. I was in no mood to lug calico and check lading bills. We were soaked through when Dolly started back to her dry stable. My mood matched the weather but Will was chipper as a soldier on payday. Feeling just as foolhardy, too, because when we met half-drowned Rufus, Will called out, "What kept you?"

"I stopped off to take torture lessons from the Injuns," Rufus answered.

His tone sobered Will considerable. He turned to watch Rufus shuffling toward the landing.

"Why is it when anyone mentions grizzly I always think of Rufus? We'd better steer clear of him for a while, Quince."

"Or stick close together." Even with Will beside me, the thought of meeting Rufus made me more than a mite uneasy. Then I remembered Will planned to go to Fort Leavenworth with the volunteers. I'd be the one left in Rufus's reach.

I dropped Will off at the Independence House, stabled Dolly, and ducked into the back of the store. As I shucked my coat in the storeroom I heard Pa telling a customer we were fresh out of gunpowder. First off I thought my hearing had gone bad. Not only did we keep plenty of gunpowder on hand with more coming upriver all summer, but I was looking right at more than forty kegs while Pa told the customer there was none to be had until our next shipment. I hurried into the store just as the door closed behind the customer.

Before I could call him back, Pa asked, "Did you get the letter read?"

"I forgot." I sprinted past him to the door.

"Quincy, come back here and give an account of yourself."

I stared at him, too surprised to worry about one lost sale. It wasn't like Pa to shout orders at me, let alone raise a fuss over something small as Uncle Fritz's letter.

"It's all right, Quince," he said softly. "I just wanted to stop you calling him back. That was Governor Armijo's brother. I'm not selling him gunpowder to cart back to Santa Fé."

"Do you think we'll fight there too?"

"It's in Mexico. Maybe we should post a guard here at night." He thought a minute, then shook his head. "No, that would just make him curious over what we're guarding."

I thought Pa was making too much of it, but when I picked up the dry goods next day, two Mexicans lounged against the pilings. They showed interest in nothing but gun cases and wooden kegs, gunpowder size. We were due for a shipment any day. I meant to warn Pa that Armijo would know when and how much gunpowder we received, but I forgot. After Mr. Mueller translated the letter from Mama's baby brother, I could think of nothing but getting Uncle Fritz's news to Pa fast as I could push old Dolly.

2
My Uncle's Keeper

"Why does he want to come here?" I asked. We'd been so busy in the store there'd been no chance to talk about Uncle Fritz until we'd had supper at the crowded hotel table and started walking home. "Mama isn't here. Why is he coming now?"

"Why do those come?" Pa pointed at the sky glow of the wagon campfires. "Why did others before them come to Virginia and New England? They're all scratching the same itch."

I was suffering an almighty itch myself, but it wasn't quite the same. I had no urge to clear land or build houses. Just seeing what lay beyond the prairie and over the mountains would satisfy me.

Pa opened the door. I stepped inside the house and waited until he lit a candle.

"I wonder what Uncle Fritz is like," I said.

"A sweet little boy, your ma always said."

"But she hadn't seen him for nearly twenty years. He's bound to have changed some."

Pa chuckled. "We'll welcome him no matter what, for your ma's sake."

I lit a candle stub from the one Pa held. "I suppose I'll have to give up my room and bed."

"Don't fret over the best way to cook rabbit till you've caught one. That letter was written before winter set in. Plenty could have happened to change his mind."

The next few days I thought every stranger coming in the store must be Uncle Fritz, but they were all easterners scratching the itch to see California or Oregon. Pa wasted a lot of time giving advice. Few of them could understand why a couple extra ax heads, kegs of powder, or sacks of beans should replace their wife's good china. Hadn't they always driven to town for their needs?

If there were youngsters in the family, often as not Pa would slip in an extra measure of beans and rice. I just piled up what they ordered and didn't argue. I had trouble myself when it came to picturing thousands of miles of nothing.

Will Dayton and Les Young barged in, all het up about joining the Missouri volunteers. Course, their enlistments wouldn't be official till they passed muster at Fort Leavenworth and were sworn in. Will bought a felt hat and an Indian band to trim it. They asked me to help them buy horses but Pa couldn't spare me. A shipment had come upriver in the morning, but we were so rushed I didn't get started to the landing until late

16

afternoon. The load was too heavy for Dolly, so I rented the livery stable's snowplow team.

Not far from town I met a wagon built higher, wider, and boxier than a Conestoga. A trader's wagon loaded with goods bought on credit from the outfitters downriver. As we drew closer I recognized Cy Petry driving. I stopped the team and waited for the big covered wagon to pull up beside me.

"Howdy, Quince." Cy asked after Pa, then said, "Is Possible still around?"

"He should be. You're the first one through this year."

"I won't be the last, by a long shot. You should see the wagons outfitting in St. Louis. Thicker than ants around a jam pot and all raring to hit Santa Fé before our boys take it and the prices fall."

"Has the army been ordered to take Santa Fé?"

"Haven't you heard? Colonel Kearny's going to be made general so he can lead the Missouri volunteers against Santa Fé. General Wool's been ordered to take Chihuahua, and old General Taylor's going slam bang to Mexico City. Put that in your hat and cogitate." His whip cracked over the team and the eight mules strained forward. "I have eleven wagons this year. If you know any drivers, send them around."

"I will." I watched the wagon lurch past, wondering if driving eight mules was much different from handling two horses. If Possible would speak a good word for me, I might ask for one of those driving jobs myself. Not that I especially wanted to be glued to a wagon seat, but it was one way of scratching my itch.

17

Cy leaned out around the high wagon top and called back, "I almost forgot. There was a Dutchie on the boat asking after your pa."

Often as not Dutchie meant German. That would be Uncle Fritz for sure. I found him perched on our shipment, the tails of his black frock coat spread carefully over the flour barrel. He wore a funny stiff black hat with a stovepipe crown. I couldn't decide if the narrow brim curled up at the sides from getting wet or if it was meant to look that way. As I jumped down, Uncle Fritz stood up and I couldn't help grinning. Mama's baby brother stood head and shoulders over me with width to match.

"Uncle Fritz?" I held out my hand expecting him to pump it and bellow *Wie geht's* the way Mr. Mueller did.

He bowed stiffly and said, "Fritz Vanderbeck."

"John Quincy Heffendorf," I answered, with a bow of my own. "Mostly called Quincy on account of Pa's name is John too."

"Your father is well?"

"*Ja.*"

"Good." He bobbed his head in another quick bow. "To speak the English is in order."

"Yes, sir." Though his English was so thick I didn't think his German would be much harder to understand. "I better check this load out. I'll be right back."

He had me so flustered with his bowing and stiff manners that I forgot to make sure he understood. He must have, because when I got back, he'd shed his frock coat and tall hat and was lifting barrels onto the wagon. That warmed me to Uncle Fritz right off.

The steamboat's mate grumbled about things being loaded without his say-so, but it checked out all right: flour, gunpowder, salt, sugar, beans, rice, and a dozen rifles. I signed the papers and helped Uncle Fritz finish loading. He lifted and I stacked. And that's when my warm feelings toward him cooled considerable. He took on so about everything being packed neat and tight in the wagon that I finally gave up hurrying and did it his way. It seemed a waste of time when we weren't hauling china or other breakables.

For himself, Uncle Fritz had only one worn leather bag and two wooden crates. He was traveling light for someone moving halfway around the world.

When he climbed up, the wagon springs grated and I had to brace myself to keep from sliding down against him. Likely the seat would have a permanent slant, but I figured someday he'd drive the wagon and it would even out.

As we pulled away, Uncle Fritz pointed at two Mexicans hustling toward horses on the bank. "Those are Indians?"

"Course not." I wouldn't have been surprised if he'd asked if they were soldiers. Most all Mexicans wore dirty white pants and loose squared-off shirts topped by wide-brimmed hats. But Indians! "Whatever gave you that notion?"

After sifting a peck of his backwards English, I caught the general idea. The Mexicans had kept sidling up to our shipment. Uncle Fritz had added the knives at their belts to their dark, unfriendly faces and come up with Indian.

"They're just Mexicans," I explained. Pa could expect another visit from Armijo.

"They are friends?"

"No, just interested in gunpowder."

I didn't feel up to explaining about Governor Armijo, Santa Fé, and the Missouri volunteers. Nor did I think Uncle Fritz could swallow it all in one chunk. He had enough strangeness to get used to. I got an idea just how much when we drove into town.

"What is this?" Uncle Fritz thundered.

"What is what?" I looked around, expecting a whiskey-fired Indian trying to relive the past. Everything looked the same as usual. Wagons, buggies, men, horses, and mules jostled for passage. Indians stood like blanket-covered rocks and let the crowd flow around them.

"The street." Uncle Fritz waved his hand at the mud-spattered buildings. "Where is the . . . the . . ."

"Paving?" He nodded and I explained: "We haven't got around to that. Haven't even thought about it that I know. The mud's not bad in winter and in the summer everyone keeps their front windows shuttered."

"Always your mother wrote this is a city."

"It is! Independence is the biggest, busiest city on the Missouri."

"It is not a city." He ran off a long, jumbled list of the things a city should have. He must have been right about the German cities, but he could have been wrong about New Orleans, only I couldn't prove it. I'd never been out of walking distance of Independence. Will Dayton had gone East to school, but he'd never talked any about paved streets, night watchmen, or city councils.

"It *is* a city," I told him. "You should have seen it ten, twelve years ago. Weren't more than five buildings and four of those were farmhouses."

He just stared at me. His wide face flushed, then got darker and darker as if he was building a head of steam like the paddle wheelers. When he was nearing the color of red flannel, two ragged men tumbled out of a tavern, wrastling and rolling between wheels and hoofs.

"Stop!" shouted Uncle Fritz. A horse shied at the fighters and dumped his rider in the mud. "Where is the police?"

"Why do we need the police? Nobody's getting hurt." I'd stopped the team so as not to run over them, and far as I could see, the men weren't even doing each other much damage.

"There must be order," said Uncle Fritz. "Every man cannot do his own wishes."

"Why not? It's a free country."

"Free!" His red face took on a purple tinge, but before he exploded, Les and Will galloped toward us. Their horses wove between wagons and jumped the pair of brawlers, which put an end to the fight. As Will and Les pulled up beside our wagon, they whooped and fired their rifles in the air.

"Dunderheads," roared Uncle Fritz. "Are you outlaws that you wish to kill us?"

21

"These are my friends," I shouted back at him.

"And your friends are free to kill you?"

"They weren't shooting *at* us." I quick passed out names. Will and Les gave Uncle Fritz a salute which didn't seem to please him any.

"How do we look?" Les asked me.

"Like sure enough soldiers."

Uncle Fritz made a gurgling noise.

Will frowned. "What do you think of this horse? It's the best I could do. Les went and blabbed our personal affairs to the only horse trader in town that didn't know Pa owned the Independence House."

"Now, Will, that trader was just being neighborly," Les said.

"He was fixing to skin us right down to our birthday suits. After Les told him who I was, this nag was the only horse in Independence I could afford."

"It looks sound to me," I told him, though all I knew about horses came from old Dolly.

Will patted its shoulder. "I hope so. If it doesn't pass muster in Fort Leavenworth, they'll send me home."

"When do you leave?"

"Day after tomorrow," Les said. "No more farm and no more plow. Whooo-eeee!"

The yelp brought Uncle Fritz up off the seat.

"You'll have to excuse him, sir," Will said. "He's still very much the innocent."

Les didn't seem to mind, but Will's eastern school talk always left me with the suspicion somebody had been insulted.

22

"The innocent what?" I asked.

"Farm boy."

"Not anymore I ain't." Les pushed his hat low over his eyes and propped his free hand on his hip.

Will grinned and shook his head. "The town is sending us off in style tomorrow night. Everybody's invited."

The last was addressed to Uncle Fritz. His nod was closer to a bow. I promised to be there. Les gave another Injun yell as he and Will wheeled and raced off, nearly spilling their horses in the slippery mud. I drove down the alley and pulled up behind the store.

My yell brought Pa out, eager to hear the why and how of Uncle Fritz's journey, but after bowing and shaking hands, Mama's baby brother said, "Everything in order. First the work, then the talk."

He shucked his coat, folded it seam to seam and laid it over the seat. He centered his hat on the coat, then started unloading the wagon. Pa stared at me.

"He's strong on order," I said.

Pa shook his head and returned to the customers. I didn't get a breather until everything was checked twice and piled neat as block matches in the storeroom. I tried to explain nothing stayed there long enough to bother, but Uncle Fritz didn't pay no mind. By the time he finished, every crate and barrel stack looked neat as if it had been fresh poured from a mold.

I wasn't overjoyed when Pa told me to take him over to the hotel for supper, but when we met Rufus Purdy, I was mighty glad to have Uncle Fritz hulking close beside me.

23

Rufus grinned like a horse about to nip, glanced up at Uncle Fritz's shoulders, and said, "I've been missing you, Quince. We have to get together real soon, just you and me."

I turned and watched him shoulder through the crowd and enter Webster's Dry Goods.

"He is a friend?" asked Uncle Fritz.

"Sort of."

"Then why does he not buy from your father?"

"His trade's no loss to Pa. Besides, it's a free country."

That set him off like the Missouri in spring flood. And not in German.

"Free for what? To shoot guns? To run down persons in the street? Look at this." He waved at the street where men were stopping to listen. "For who is this freedom? I tell you. It is for dunderheads and donkeys."

None of the staring men said anything, but they looked the way I'd felt when I put Rufus out of the wagon.

"Come on." I grabbed Uncle Fritz's arm and hauled him away. He brushed off my hand. I feared he'd turn back to preach some more, but he tugged down his vest, straightened his frock coat, and followed me into the hotel.

Folks at the long board table greeted us friendly enough, then men who'd heard Uncle Fritz in the street drifted in, spotted Mama's baby brother, and whispered to their neighbors. As the story went round the table, talk at our end fell off. With all the hard looks passed our way, I didn't breathe easy till we got back to the store.

Uncle Fritz couldn't help customers, what with the money being different and most of the paper packets having words he couldn't read, but he went right to work stacking and lining things up. I took Pa to one side and told him what had happened.

"If he talks like that again, there's bound to be trouble," I finished.

"It's the war," Pa said. "Folks are worked up like it was '76 all over again. Why, even the Purdy boy is volunteering."

"Rufus Purdy?" I couldn't believe it. "Who told you that?"

"He did. He was in here not ten minutes ago buying rifles."

"Rifles? What does he need with more than one?"

"He was buying for a couple other boys. They were out rounding up horses and gear."

"I didn't know there were two people in Independence fool enough to trust a Purdy with hard money."

Pa grinned. "Must be. Rufus paid cash over the counter."

Three Independence ladies came in for flour, full of talk about the pies they were baking for the send-off the next night. Pa would end up donating the flour and maybe the sugar as well. It rubbed me to think it would feed Rufus. I couldn't understand him enlisting after the way he'd talked against the army. And even if two other volunteers had trusted him to buy rifles, where had Rufus gotten the money for his own? Not from that one mangy buffalo robe. And if he had cash, why hadn't he bought the guns while he was at Webster's Dry Goods?

"I'll be right back," I called to Pa and hightailed it over to Webster's. Rufus had bought guns there, too. He'd paid cash for two pistols and an old Hawkins muzzle-loader.

"He's buying guns for Armijo," I told Pa. "Nobody will sell to the Mexican traders, so they're using Rufus."

Pa didn't believe me. He took it that Rufus and his friends wanted to be sure they weren't caught with empty guns. A lot could happen to a man while he loaded his rifle for a second shot.

"Rufus is no fool. He knows anyone caught buying guns for Armijo is likely to be strung to the nearest tree," Pa added. "With the volunteers leaving, folks aren't thinking quite straight."

"I know." I watched Uncle Fritz untangle ribbons. I was still thinking of Rufus, but Pa must have thought I was worrying over Uncle Fritz.

"We'll have to stick close and keep him out of trouble, for your ma's sake." Pa reached up and turned out the hanging lanterns. "Come along, Fritz. We'll go home, boil up some coffee, and have a talk."

We didn't learn much, just that we were the last of Uncle Fritz's kin, even by way of marriage, and he'd been planning on joining us since before Mama died. Now he was here, ready to start working again at his trade. He looked so much like a blacksmith or a wagon builder that I'd forgot he'd been apprenticed to a clock-maker when he was ten.

Pa looked doubtful. "You might have to turn your hand to something else, Fritz."

"I am a clockmaker," he said. "My mark on a clock has meaning. That is what I know and that is what I do."

I hoped the word wouldn't get out until after Will and Les left town. They'd never let me live down a barn-sized uncle who fiddled with the innards of a clock.

Mostly Uncle Fritz talked about Mama. He asked a dozen times if she'd been happy in this place. The way he said it put my back up. He made it sound like Pa had forced Mama to live a hard life that wore her out before her time. It hadn't been that way at all. Pa kept telling him how happy Mama had been, always singing and laughing, working at church socials and quilting bees when there'd finally been enough folks in Independence for such things.

"You think I'd have kept her here if she hadn't liked it much as I did?" Pa's voice sounded the way it had the time Will and me nearly got Les drowned on a makeshift raft.

"She could not like it," Uncle Fritz insisted. "It is not . . . not . . ."

"Not what she was accustomed to?" Pa supplied. "It's different, I'll grant you that. And a mite rough at times, but she liked it. You will too if you give it half a chance."

Uncle Fritz's look dared Pa to prove it.

Pa shoved back his empty cup. "Time we all got some sleep."

Just as I'd figured, Uncle Fritz got my lean-to. He offered to share the bed, but from the size of him I didn't think there'd be enough room left for me to balance on. I bedded down on the braided rug in front of the fireplace. I hadn't tried it since the days when Will and me played Indian scouts, but Possible slept there regular. What with the rug and the quilts it was comfortable enough, but I couldn't get to sleep.

I still thought Rufus worked for Armijo, but I didn't want to stir folks up against him without proof. There was an outside chance Pa was right. Tomorrow night the volunteers would ride to the farewell social together. If Rufus was among them, I'd swallow my suspicions.

I woke to rattle and thuds and the mumbled cussing of someone trying to be quiet. I pushed aside the quilts. In the dim light I made out Possible hunched over the fireplace.

"That coffee and bacon smells good," I said. "Is there enough for two?"

Possible turned and stared at me from swollen red eyes. "I thought you'd growed out of playing Injun."

"Uncle Fritz came from Germany. He has my room."

The trapper rubbed his matted beard. "Would he be the Dutchie what called us stupid jackasses?"

" 'Dunderheads and donkeys' is what he said. How do you know?"

"Bad news spreads like a prairie fire." He pushed

28

slabs of bacon onto two plates, added thick slices of bread, and passed one plate to me. When he handed me the cup, his hand shook so bad the coffee slopped over and scalded my wrist. I tried not to show it hurt.

"You look awful," I said.

"Ain't nothing to how I feel."

"Then why do you drink so blamed much?"

"Why does an Injun risk his hide to count coup?"

Going on a tear seemed a poor way to show courage, but I kept my thoughts to myself. Pa came out and accepted Possible's offer to help in the store until Cy Petry's wagons pulled out. That, Pa said, would leave me free to dog Uncle Fritz and keep him out of trouble. I wouldn't have half minded the job if Uncle Fritz hadn't worked me to a frazzle.

All morning I toted water from the rain barrel and set it to boil, then helped Uncle Fritz scrub and polish till I thought my arms would drop off. When we finished the house was as spotless as when Mama was living but it didn't look the same. Everything was too right. The benches set square with the table, the dishes lined up as even as regular soldiers, and the bed covers hung straight as if they'd been drawn with a straight edge. It didn't look like a house that was used to people.

While I cleaned myself to match the house, Uncle Fritz rummaged in one of his cases and brought out a carved wooden clock. He hung it on the wall, pulled down the weights, and then moved the minute hand. When it reached the hour, a small door opened and a bird popped out.

29

Uncle Fritz smiled at me. "How is that?"

"Fine except you got the bird singing backwards. It should go bob*white*, bob*white*."

He flushed angrily. "Everything here is out of order. People shoot at friends. Now the cuckoo should go 'bob*white*.'"

I shut up and watched him set the clock to noon. The bird popped out to call every hour.

"Mama would have liked that."

"*Ja*, at home we had a big one with two birds. One for the center of the hour, but only the small ones could I carry."

"You brought more of these?"

"*Ja*, for selling in your father's store."

I shook my head. "I don't think you'll sell many. Folks heading west are getting rid of clocks, not buying them."

"These are good clocks. Everything is in balance."

He was turning color again, so I let it go. While Pa and Possible went out for dinner, Uncle Fritz and I hung four of his clocks in the store and set them running.

"Don't that beat all," said Possible when he heard them.

Pa just shook his head.

As the afternoon wore on, more and more people crowded into the store to hear the cuckoos. When Uncle Fritz realized they'd come to listen and not to buy, his face grew long as Pa's. We hadn't been able to set all four clocks exactly together and at seven o'clock

30

cuckoos kept singing till Pa ordered them all stopped but one.

"It's enough to drive a man daft," he grumbled.

But we were lucky to have them. Not selling those clocks kept Uncle Fritz so worried he paid no mind to the talk going on around him.

We needn't have worried about closing at eight. Even the emigrants were caught up in the party for the volunteers. Plank tables had been set up in the space between the smithy and the stable. Women gossiped as they arranged the pies. The fiddlers sat in a wagon bed decorated with the town's Fourth of July bunting. They tuned up for the dance while we waited for the parade. Pa spied Mr. Mueller in the crowd and took Uncle Fritz over to meet him. They were still *wie geht's*-ing and bowing when we heard the drums. Everyone pressed back to make room for the horses.

Les rode first, grinning from ear to ear as he pounded a marching beat on two Indian tom-toms tied to his saddle. He waved to me and missed a beat, but it didn't matter. The volunteers were riding back and forth, stopping to greet friends, waving and grinning at the cheers. I kept looking for Rufus, but with the confusion and the dim torchlight, I couldn't even find Will. The volunteers sorted themselves into three rows in front of the wagon bed platform, their backs to the crowd.

Pa had an eye on Uncle Fritz, who was listening to Mr. Mueller explain the volunteers. There didn't seem to be any harm in moving closer to the platform. I

31

hadn't gone a dozen steps when I heard Mr. Mueller bellowing in German. I turned, but everyone else was trying to get closer too. Suddenly the crowd pushed back. I shoved forward and stumbled into a circle cleared for a fight.

Mr. Mueller hopped around, waving his fists and yelling in German. If he calmed enough to switch to English, he wasn't going to be the only one fighting mad. Uncle Fritz just stood there rubbing his cheek and calling for police while Pa kept fending off Mr. Mueller and trying to reason with him. I moved in to help, and Pa shoved Uncle Fritz at me.

"Get him out of here before he gets himself killed," he ordered.

Only Uncle Fritz didn't want to leave and he was too big for me to drag.

"You're the only kin we got left," I told him. "You want us to lose you soon as you get here? What would Mama say?"

He stopped carrying on about law and order and followed me. While Mr. Mueller gave the crowd Uncle Fritz's opinion of the volunteer army, I led Mama's sweet little baby brother around the stable and down the alley. I figured to keep to the alley all the way to Murphy's Tavern before I risked crossing the street to get home. As we neared the back of the store, Uncle Fritz grabbed my shoulder.

"Halt!" He peered ahead. "Listen."

At first I heard only the noise of the crowd behind us. Then in the short silences I heard a barrel rolling on a wooden floor. A mule wheezed and harness jingled before cheers again drowned all sound from the alley. As we moved quietly forward I could just make out the tall dark shape of a wagon. Two wagons, drawn up single file behind Pa's store. The rear door opened. Light flared into the alley. It was quickly shielded but not before it showed us men in wide Mexican hats rolling kegs from our storeroom to the farthest wagon.

"Thief! Outlaw!" roared Uncle Fritz.

He charged like a mad bull. I didn't waste breath yelling. I clenched my fists, lowered my head, and waded in.

3

My Uncle's Partner

The first Mexican I hit went down easy. He sprang to his feet and ran for the wagon he'd been loading. I didn't bother chasing him. There were plenty more running in all directions, mostly away from swinging, bellowing Uncle Fritz. One ran for the near wagon and made a try for the driver's seat. All I could make out was the blur of his white shirt and pants, but it was enough to show he was more Uncle Fritz's size game than mine. Just the same, I couldn't let him get away with that wagon.

I lowered my head and rammed his back. He let out a grunt and before he caught his wind, I wrapped both arms around his waist and pulled. He came down on top, kicking and clawing at my gripped hands. I'd caught myself between a rock and a hard place. I couldn't roll him under me, I didn't dare let go, and his big hat squashed against my face was about to smother me.

He gave up on my hands, reached back over his head and felt under the hat for my eyes. I figured I was done for, but that oversized brim kept getting in his way. When his thumb slid over my mouth, I bit down hard. He yelled and broke free.

He must've jumped clean to his feet because I was hardly rid of the hat when his boot came at my head. It scared me so bad I couldn't think straight. I just grabbed the swinging leg and held on. My left shoulder and hip plowed up the alley as he tried to kick me loose. I collected a mess of bruises and even keeping my neck tight against the thick leg didn't protect my face altogether. Suddenly he froze and I heard the creak of heavy wheels. The loaded wagon was pulling out.

"You stinking cowards," yelled my thief.

"Rufus!" There was no mistaking that hoarse, raspy voice.

The surprise loosened my hold. He pulled free. I rolled, covering my head with my arms, but the fight was over. I looked up in time to see his white shirt disappear inside the back of the fleeing wagon.

As I picked myself up and felt for broken bones, the alley flickered with light. Uncle Fritz's roars had finally gotten through to the men at the social. Their torches showed one abandoned wagon, scattered gunpowder kegs and five Mexicans laid out on the ground at Uncle Fritz's feet.

"Thief! Vandal!" Uncle Fritz shouted. "Who keeps the order? Where is the police?"

"Don't worry. We'll catch them," said one of the

men. "Jake, send a couple boys over to Armijo's camp. If that wagon isn't there, wait till it shows up."

Pa strode up and looked over the scene. "Possible?"

The old trapper moved into the light.

"Better unhitch those mules and take them to the livery stable for now." Pa watched me rub my shoulder. I must have looked as bad as I felt. "Fritz will help him, Quince. We'll check the stores."

The unconscious Mexicans were dragged off to jail. Men rolled the scattered kegs back up the planks into the storeroom.

Possible grinned at me. "How come I missed the fun?"

"You'd have been welcome to my share," I told him. "I can't put a finger anywhere that doesn't hurt."

"Are you telling this old hoss that a Mexican toed up to a fight?"

I touched the scraped side of my face and winced. "That was no Mexican. That was Rufus Purdy."

The men holding the torches turned around.

"You sure?" one asked.

"I couldn't mistake that voice."

"Voice! Didn't you see him?"

"Well, no. It was dark and he had his back to me the whole time. Except there at the end when I was in no position to do any stargazing."

The men laughed. Even Possible grinned.

"Nobody could mess you like that with his back to you," someone pointed out.

"He weren't fighting," said someone else. "He got mule kicked."

"I wasn't kicked. I fought!" My voice was near as loud as Uncle Fritz's. "And I fought Rufus Purdy."

None of them spoke for so long I started fidgeting. Finally one said, "You better be careful naming names without proof."

"You prove it wasn't Rufus. He told Pa he was joining the volunteers. Is he back there with them?"

Nobody remembered seeing Rufus. They decided to check his whereabouts. In a moment there was no one in the darkened alley but Possible, Uncle Fritz and me. I went inside and helped Pa total the loss. Two barrels of flour and seventeen kegs of gunpowder were missing from the storeroom. They must have been emptying the gun case when they heard Uncle Fritz yell, dropped their loads and run. Under the scattered guns we found a broken cuckoo clock.

Pa stared at it thoughtfully, then said, "Let's get these guns back in the case so I can see what's missing."

Armijo was ahead two new percussion rifles, a brace of pistols and the old rifle I'd fancied, the one with buffalo heads decorating the stock. It gave me a turn to think it might be pointed at Will or Les.

Uncle Fritz lumbered in. He knelt and carefully gathered the pieces of the clock one by one.

"The mules are all stabled?" Pa asked.

"*Ja.*"

"Where's Possible?"

"He returned." Uncle Fritz jerked his head in the direction of the social. He rose, holding the bits of clock carefully. "Such a thing should not happen."

I couldn't tell if he meant smashing the clock or

breaking into the store. Just the same, it riled me. After his talk with Mr. Mueller, he must know we were fixing to go to war. With Armijo camped right outside town, what did he expect?

"You should look on that broken clock as a compliment," Pa said. "One of those Mexicans liked it well enough to steal."

"Maybe it is to Mexico I should go."

"That's a good idea," I said. "You'd like Santa Fé."

Pa glared at me, but Uncle Fritz perked up.

"Santa Fé is a city?"

"Biggest city in New Mexico." I didn't mention it was the only one. "It's hundreds of years old. Anyways, older than anything in this country."

He looked so interested I warmed up to my story and stretched the truth a mite more. "It's got a governor and I hear tell he's got soldiers to keep order."

Uncle Fritz looked at Pa. "Why did you not take my sister to this city?"

"Because it's a foreign country." Pa was closer to exploding than I'd ever seen him. "And just remember it was probably some of Armijo's so-called soldiers that broke in here tonight. That's how much he cares for law and order."

Pa must have noticed Uncle Fritz's flush at the way he'd said "foreign country," 'cause he changed his tone to say, "Maybe one of us should sleep here in case they come back."

"*Nein,* that is not the way. Everything must be done in order. You keep the store. The police keep guard."

He turned dark pink telling us how to organize

Independence so we'd have law and order. I'd become an expert on Uncle Fritz's order fever. He could be shouted down in the pink stage or headed off when turning red. But when he hit crimson and fell back into German, nothing but force or fire would stop him. He was nearing the last stage before I thought to groan and slide to the floor.

Pa reached me first. I winked at him and said weakly, "I must be hurt worse than I thought."

"We'll take you home."

Uncle Fritz wouldn't have it. "First you get the doctor."

Pa and I looked at each other helplessly. All Uncle Fritz needed was to hear we had no doctor in Independence. There might be one with the emigrants, but usually there was something badly wrong with a doctor moving west.

"Everyone's at the social," I said at last, hoping he'd think that's where the doctor was.

"Then we take you there."

"Pa needs you to fix the back door." There's nothing harder than acting just the right amount of sick. I got up and swayed a little, hoping I hadn't overdone it. "I can make it all right."

Pa played along, clucking and acting doubtful, then deciding I could manage the short walk by myself. They let me out the front door. I didn't hear it close, so I walked like a clubbed mule till I was out of sight.

The ruckus at the store had dampened the party spirit, but it picked up again when I limped into the torchlight. The volunteers crowded around and treated me as something of a hero. Will pointed out I was the first one in Independence to fight the enemy. My skinned face and ragged clothes proved it. The way the girls giggled and fussed over me, I figured on asking Sue Ellen Hodges to dance if and when the fiddling started. There'd been some talk about calling off the social, but they decided an attack by the enemy here in town made it even more important to send the boys off right.

Lou Blakely, who was thinking of running for Congress, got up on the decorated wagon bed. He made a thundering speech, starting way back at the Alamo, working through the Mexicans forcing Texans to draw for black beans, and winding up with Mexico's hasty and unprovoked declaration of war, though I couldn't help but feel General Taylor might have prodded them a mite.

"Our brothers' blood cries from the ground," Lou finished. "And Missouri answers! Her sons shall charge the gates of Santa Fé as Ethan Allen stormed the gates of Ticonderoga!"

By the time Will's father presented a flag and told the volunteers to defend it with their blood, everyone was hoarse with cheering and ready to celebrate.

The fiddlers struck up a foot-stomping tune and the volunteers grabbed all the girls. After considerable maneuvering I managed to be alongside Sue Ellen when she finished a reel. Before I could get a word out, she swung off with Hank Fletcher, who was all of twenty-two and wore a beard. None of the dancers so much as glanced my way. A couple of windy speeches and nobody remembered I'd just fought a battle on our home ground. Not that I'd won or even struck as big a blow as Uncle Fritz, but it did seem folks had awful short memories. Especially Sue Ellen.

I waited until the men came back from chasing the thieves. According to his uncle, Rufus had packed up and left on business of his own. All the Mexican wagons had disappeared. They'd try again come daylight, but there were too many gulleys and thickets where a wagon could be hidden and everyone was too busy to track them far. No one from Missouri would see that gunpowder again unless they got in firing distance of the Mexicans. It was a disheartening thought to take home to bed.

When the volunteers rode out next morning we all lined up in front of the store to watch. I waved and yelled good-bye to Will and Les, but they couldn't hear over the cheers going up along the street.

"Scarecrows and dunderheads," said Uncle Fritz. "A dunderhead army that cannot ride in line."

There was plenty more, but it came out in double time mixed with so much German I couldn't follow it.

"That's enough, Fritz." Pa's voice was low, but something in it cut Uncle Fritz off in midgrunt. He jerked down his vest and stomped into the store.

"Are you sure he's kin to your missus?" asked Possible.

Pa sighed. "It's a good thing nobody heard him."

After the fight last night the townfolks had decided to overlook Uncle Fritz's first opinions, but that didn't mean they'd forgotten. All morning kin to the volun-

41

teers had been coming into the store asking how long the Dutchie planned to stay. Some asked plain out when he was leaving.

"Another one of his speeches and little Fritz will be about as popular as a skunk in a sweat bath," Possible said.

Pa rocked back and forth on his heels. "Maybe we ought to get him out of Independence for a spell."

"He's pretty riled over that broken clock," I said. "You might give him old Dolly and a gun and sic him onto Armijo. Just getting to Santa Fé and back would take him all summer."

Pa stopped rocking. "That's what I had in mind. He's been pestering Possible about Santa Fé all morning."

"Pa! I was only fooling. He'd get lost and starve or get picked off by Comanches. You think Mama would like that?"

"No, but nothing like that would happen if he joined a train and you went with him."

"*Me!*"

Possible grinned like an idiot, but Pa looked all business.

"But, Pa, thirty miles out on the prairie and I'll be just as raw as Uncle Fritz. The Comanches will get two scalps instead of one. Right, Possible?"

The trapper looked thoughtful. "That's possible, but there's no danger from Injuns this side of Council Grove. Join a good train there and you're most sure to keep your hair. And you ain't as green as you think, Quince. I taught you to cook rations and read enough

42

sign to keep on the trail far as Council Grove. After that it don't matter. Might be you could even shoot game, providing it's deaf and lame."

That last was close enough to the truth that I let it pass. "Any greenhorn can do that much."

"Not your Uncle Fritz," said Pa. "He can't drive a team, tend mules or make camp. And the way he rubs folks, nobody's going to help him if he makes a mistake."

"That's certain," said Possible.

"Anyways," Pa went on, "I'm not sending you on a chase for our stolen goods. Armijo left us one wagon and team. I've been persuaded to keep them even though they're worth a bit more than Armijo stole. Since Fritz has showed such an interest in Santa Fé, I thought I'd set him up in the trade."

"Good idea," I agreed. "But why send me?"

"To keep him alive. Your ma would never rest easy if we let anything happen to her baby brother. You saw Mr. Mueller last night. The same thing could happen a dozen times on the trail."

"That's possible," put in the trapper, "but I'd say he'd be more likely to meet with a gun, knife, or some other little accident after the second time."

Pa must have followed my thoughts because he added, "And once the fighting starts and a couple volunteers get killed, the same thing may happen to Fritz here in Independence. Unless he keeps his opinions to himself, which I doubt."

"I still don't see how my going will help any." I sure

wanted to see the other side of the mountains, but something told me traveling with Uncle Fritz wasn't the way to do it. "I can't keep him from talking."

Pa smiled. "You did fine last night. You just drive the wagon to Council Grove, join a good train, and keep Fritz from socializing, especially with Americans. Keep him away from folks and he'll stay in one piece."

"Maybe." But I wasn't too sure.

Possible laughed and slapped his thigh. "If I hadn't already pledged my word to Cy Petry, dogged if I wouldn't trail along. Watching Fritz take the prairie would be more fun than a bear fight."

With Pa standing right there I couldn't tell Possible what I thought of spending six months with Uncle Fritz. When wagoners broke oxen in a hurry, they yoked a pair, tied their tails together and let them run until they either kicked each other to death or learned to work as a team. That's the way I pictured Uncle Fritz and me, only I didn't think I'd ever learn to pull in his direction and he sure wouldn't pull in mine.

The volunteers had ridden out of sight. People drifted back to their everyday affairs. Some had pushed by us to the store and were waiting for Pa, Possible or me. Only an emigrant had let Uncle Fritz wait on him and he'd given up trying to make Mama's baby brother understand sorghum molasses.

Pa went to figuring what stock he could spare for Santa Fé while Possible and I filled orders. Uncle Fritz got in everybody's way putting things to rights. He hardly waited for a woman to finish fingering calico before he had the bolt back on the shelf. Some of the

44

emigrant tykes kept getting him to say velvet so they could giggle at the way he said *v* like a *w*. They didn't do it out of meanness, but it gave me some notion of what Uncle Fritz would go through if the town turned against him. I waited on their folks quick and Pa steered Uncle Fritz to a bin of snarled twine in the back of the store.

After he finished with the twine, Uncle Fritz sorted all the whips and harness according to size and hung them over the nails so all the ends were even.

"He's worse than an Injun with a medicine ceremony," grumbled Possible. "Can't he leave anything natural?"

All his fussing did make a body jumpy. I tried to tell myself that was the only reason we weren't doing the business we should, but I didn't believe it. Not the way some folks made a point of not seeing Uncle Fritz. It all wore me down to admitting that taking Uncle Fritz to Santa Fé was the only reasonable thing to do. And when Pa threw back all my arguments about traveling, what could I do but say yes? Though nursemaiding Uncle Fritz was like scratching my itch with a bag full of fleas.

By the time we closed that night Pa had things pretty well settled in his mind. But he hadn't reckoned with Uncle Fritz.

Clockmakers made clocks and traders traded. It was not orderly for Uncle Fritz to work at another's trade. Sure, he'd like to go to Santa Fé but to make clocks, not to trade. Any rabbit brain could understand that joining the traders was the easiest and safest way to get to Santa

45

Fé, but not Uncle Fritz. He thought the trip to Santa Fé was twice as easy as getting to Independence and no one could convince him otherwise.

Pa argued through two pots of coffee. Possible lost interest early, wrapped himself in a trade blanket and stretched out in front of the fire. I slumped over the table half asleep. The first time my name came up I was too drowsy to more than grunt. After the third or fourth time I came full awake and caught the drift of Pa's newest argument. He was putting me in partnership with Uncle Fritz!

"It's high time Quincy struck out on his own," he said. "At his age, you already knew a trade. But I couldn't let him make the first trip without someone to watch over him."

Pa needn't have glared at me. I was too stunned to protest.

"Besides," he went on, "there must be a big market for clocks in Santa Fé if those Mexicans tried to steal them."

Uncle Fritz nodded. "So I have thought. But to live in Santa Fé is no better than to stay at home. I came to be with you."

"No need to stay in Santa Fé," Pa told him. "You go along with Quince, see what the market is, and then you can come back here and make clocks all winter. Quince can tote them to Santa Fé each summer."

I hoped Pa meant that. Going back and forth like Possible would suit me fine. With that ahead of me, I could put up with Uncle Fritz one trip. I grinned at him. "I reckon we're partners if you say so."

46

He brought a leather sack from his room, emptied his savings on the table and asked for the partnership terms.

"Quincy will supply the wagon, team, rations and as much of the trade goods as we can spare. If the Mexicans hold Santa Fé when you arrive, you'll have to pay fifty to a hundred per cent duty on the trade goods, then hire a go-between to sell them." Pa pushed aside most of Uncle Fritz's coins. "This should cover those expenses with a mite extra for emergencies. Use the rest to stock the wagon with things I can't spare."

"It is agreed," said Uncle Fritz. He shook hands and bowed all around.

"Don't forget those clocks," Pa added as the one on the kitchen wall cuckooed once.

We only had four hours to sleep, but Uncle Fritz took the time to cover the broken clock with a sugar sack towel. He claimed it was to keep the dirt and dust from the innards, but he acted like it was respect for the dead.

Possible slept Indian style, feet to the fire, which left me half the rug for padding. As I rolled up in the quilts it occurred to me I was getting an overdose of change and upheaval. Sleeping on the floor was the least of it.

I'd lost my best friend to the Grand Army of the West. Ahead was a journey of nearly eight hundred miles to an enemy city. I'd been made a full-fledged businessman and been saddled with a partner green as grass and overstrong on order. I could picture Uncle Fritz loose on the prairie. He'd want the snakes to stand straight on their tails and the buffalo to march by fours. Why in blazes hadn't I just let Rufus drive that second wagon away with the first one?

"Jehosephat!" I sat bolt upright.

Possible threw back his blanket and scrabbled for a gun that wasn't there before he roused enough to know where he was.

"What's the yelling for?" he asked.

"I was just thinking."

"Well, think quiet if you bed down with me." He pulled the blanket over his head, grumbling about greenhorns and false alarms.

What I'd been thinking was no false alarm. I knew blame well I'd fought Rufus Purdy behind the store. Where would he go except with Armijo?

Traders described Santa Fé as a pesthole of barbarians, a town as sinful as it was dirty. Strings of human ears hung in the jail and the people played music and danced jigs at funerals. What a place to meet Rufus, who now had two scores to settle with me. And meet him I would. There wasn't a prayer he'd move on before I arrived, not when Santa Fé suited him so well.

Blast that comet to ruination, I thought. I knew the comet had nothing to do with my fix, but it was a comfort to have something besides my own blundering to blame for what waited in Santa Fé. So I lay there cussing out Biela's comet while sweat broke out all over.

4

Eins, Zwei, Drei!

Possible crammed all the help he could into the next few days. He went over the landmarks and campsites between Independence and Council Grove until I had them memory perfect. Three rainy mornings in a row he dragged me out of the quilts before dawn, made me hitch up the eight mules, and drive that oversized wagon around all three streets of Independence. The biggest difference from driving the double-teamed snowplow was that horses obeyed the reins. Mules ran on whip crack and yell. My lung power came off better than my whip skill. The sixteen feet of lash fought back like a cross-eyed snake. Every time the whip sagged over their backs the mules twitched their ears and jerked sideways.

"Keep that lash up," Possible ordered. "Mules get fractious if it touches."

The third morning I only tipped one rain barrel and

the whip snaked out smoothly a foot over the mules' backs. The crack was more like a cork pop than a rifle shot, but at least I'd caught the knack.

Possible nodded. "You'll do, once you get out on the prairie."

After breakfast he showed Uncle Fritz and me how to waterproof the wagon. We spread two Mackinaw blankets over the patched cover already in place. Then a second layer, of Osnaburg cloth, long enough to reach the wagon bed, was pulled tight and lashed firmly in place.

"That should hold against anything 'cepting a twister." Possible winked at Uncle Fritz. "You can dis-remember those blankets till you get through Mexican customs."

"*Nein*, the tax we pay."

"You'll pay plenty without adding two prime Mackinaws."

"We pay for all. Good streets, police, city council, law and order are by taxes."

"That's possible, but I don't think them things is what Governor Armijo has in mind."

"We pay," thundered Uncle Fritz. "It is better to pay than have thief and vandals. In the streets is mud and dunderheads with guns."

Bellowing from the back of the wagon, he was likely to collect everyone passing the end of the alley. I figured the best way to steer Uncle Fritz from one kind of disorder was to give him another kind to stew over.

I said loud and clear, "Possible, you pile up the trade goods and I'll throw them in the wagon."

50

That chopped off Uncle Fritz's favorite sermon, but I added for good measure, "We'll start with the crates of cuckoo clocks."

The tail end of the wagon rose a foot as Uncle Fritz jumped down. "To pack in order everything must first be gathered."

Possible and I agreed to pile all the trade goods beside the wagon while Uncle Fritz worked out the best way to stow them in the wagon.

With '46 looking to be the biggest year in Independence history we couldn't strip the store. Some of what Pa could spare, Governor Armijo wouldn't allow in Santa Fé. Guns, lead and powder made up a good part of any trader's goods, but anything warlike except knives was on Pa's forbidden list, though he'd promised guns for our own use.

We scraped together yard goods, shawls, ribbons, axes and knives, looking glasses, pen cases and paper, needles, and just plain iron that Uncle Fritz bought because Possible swore it brought better than two dollars a pound in Santa Fé. Piled beside the wagon, along with Uncle Fritz's cuckoo clocks, it made a good showing. But when Uncle Fritz stowed it neat and orderly in the wagon, it didn't seem enough to make the trip worth while. It wasn't anywhere near the five thousand pounds Cy Petry carried in each of his wagons. We weren't making this trip strictly for business, but it wouldn't hurt to show a profit.

While we took a breather, Possible said, "I'm bedding down by Cy's wagons tonight. We're pulling out in the morning."

That gave me a sinking feeling. We'd be able to join a wagon train in Council Grove, but I was going to miss Possible and his savvy. When it came to prairie travel I was near as green as Uncle Fritz.

"Will Cy lay over in Council Grove long enough for us to catch up?" I asked.

"It's possible, but I doubt it. Cy wants to hit Santa Fé before the army takes it and the prices fall."

My feelings must have showed.

"Don't worry, hoss," said the trapper. "We'll meet up in Santa Fé. Look out for Uncle and don't get mired in no buffler wallows."

Buffalo! The magic word conjured up all the tall tales Possible had spun during the long winters. Buffalo herds, Comanche and Kiowa, Bent's Fort and the cloud-high Rockies. I'd see them all, starting in a few days. If luck rode with us I might even get to see the battle for Santa Fé. If only I wasn't saddled with Uncle Fritz.

As I said farewell to Possible I pushed down the memory of Rufus Purdy's raspy voice. The trapper often said there weren't no use stringing trap lines till you struck beaver country. With Santa Fé eight hundred miles out of Independence I figured I had sufficient time to worry over Rufus. Right now there were problems closer to home, such as help in the store for Pa.

What with poor stock, worse wagons, too little money, and an oversupply of ignorance, there were always emigrant families forced to give up before they hardly started. When one of them dragged back to town, Pa worked out a deal for the man to help in the store.

Between customers, training the new man and Uncle Fritz's persnickety ways, it took most of three days to load our rations. I let Mama's baby brother tote the hundred pounds each of flour and bacon, but twenty pounds of coffee beans, forty pounds of sugar, some salt and two kegs of crackers put considerable strain on my own back.

The night before we left, Uncle Fritz went early to his room. Pa and me sat late before the fire talking of Mama, old times in Independence, the war and the Missouri volunteers. Finally we got around to Santa Fé.

"I'll come back in September with Possible," I promised.

"No need, Quince. By that time I'll be able to handle the store alone."

I sat hunched up by the fire. I knew there'd be no need of me to hurry back, but right then I wasn't overly anxious to leave.

Pa went on. "Once you're in Santa Fé you may as well winter over and see a bit of the country. If it's safe, that is. Then again, this war might not last long. Use your judgment, Quince. Do what you consider best all around."

That meant if the war was still going strong I should hold Uncle Fritz in Santa Fé until spring. If we two greenies ever reached Santa Fé. Eight hundred miles came out fast in words, but I knew it took months to travel. A lot could happen even to a wagon train. Pa must have known how I felt. He tussled my hair, something he hadn't done since I was a tad.

"You'll make out, son. Just keep your wits about you and don't rile Ma's baby brother more than you need to."

He rose quickly and went to his room. I stretched out in my quilts and watched the line of candlelight under the lean-to door till I fell asleep.

Uncle Fritz must have brushed and polished all night. He turned out looking like a St. Louis lawyer. His frock coat and flannel vest appeared tailor new. The rain spots hardly showed on his tall hat and his black boots shone ice slick and glossy. After we'd hitched up the team, blamed if he didn't take out a cloth and brush to slick himself up again. Then he jerked smooth his vest, settled the hat firmly on his head, shook hands with Pa and climbed to the wagon seat.

"Are you sure you can handle that team?" Pa asked me for the hundredth time.

For the hundredth time I assured him I could.

"Good luck, son." Pa hesitated, then shook my hand and clapped me on the shoulder. "Sun's up. Better get rolling."

"I'll send a letter every chance I get," I promised.

"Do that."

I climbed up beside Uncle Fritz, holding stiff to counter the tilt of the seat. I took up the whip and reins, trying to look as if I knew what I was about. Pa stepped forward and slapped the off lead mule.

"Move out," he shouted.

The oversized wagon lurched and swayed over the ruts. It was the first time I'd driven out the alley without Possible's help. The cross street came at me faster than perdition. I snaked the whip and let loose a string of words I'd heard around the stable. Uncle Fritz clawed the seat bottom as the wagon heeled over at the turn. It balanced on a prayer, then thudded back onto all four wheels.

"*Gott sei dank*," he muttered.

"Amen." In spite of a bad case of shakes, I hung over the side for a last glimpse of Pa. He ran to the end of the alley and raised his hand in farewell. The mules plodded forward with no help from me. I waved till we lurched onto the angling road out of town. As we rolled down a slope, Independence dropped away till only the top of the Independence House showed. When that was gone, I faced the prairie and tried to remember everything Possible had taught me about the route.

"First overnight stop is Round Grove," I told Uncle Fritz. "We might catch up with some wagons there."

But neither of us was used to resting and watering a team. We got in each other's way and tangled ourselves in the harness. Then there were mud holes. With everything so wet, we couldn't spot them until we were stuck. We spent most of the day spreading brush and pushing, then untangling the consarned mules. Low gray clouds and misty rain promised an early dusk. Close to four o'clock, best I could judge, I spied a likely creek and turned off for the night.

"Where is the Round Grove?" asked Uncle Fritz.

"Up ahead somewheres. We couldn't have made more than twenty miles today."

"Where do we sleep? What is to eat?"

"We eat our rations and sleep as best we can." He

looked puzzled, so I explained. "Those provisions we packed the last three days are our trail rations."

"The fat and flour are to trade."

"They are to eat." There was no question of who'd have to cook. I wondered if I dared trust Uncle Fritz with the mules. For sure I couldn't do everything.

"Can you handle the team?" I asked. "Water them at the creek, then stake them out. Be sure to get the picket pins deep. Possible says the first five or six days the stock tries to get back to Independence."

With the little distance we'd put between town and ourselves the mules wouldn't have much of a run if they pulled stakes.

Using the drier underbranches of a deadfall along the creek, I got a fire started and stacked damp wood behind it to dry. I found the grinder tucked between the sacks of coffee beans and decided there was something to be said for Uncle Fritz's order. But I forgot what it was when I took the coffee pot down to the creek for water.

Uncle Fritz was staking out mule number three. I should have known he'd line them up neat and orderly with never a thought as to whether their grazing circles would overlap and tangle their ropes. But he'd sure enough set the picket pins deep. I thought we'd have to hitch up a team to get them out. By the time we'd pulled and reset two of the stakes my fire was out.

It was full dark before I mixed the biscuits and set the skillet on edge near the fire to bake. I was muddy, wet and wore out. Only the mouth-watering smell of frying salt pork and the promise of hot coffee kept me awake.

Uncle Fritz hunkered down by the fire. I set the pans of biscuits and salt pork between us, put the sugar close to hand and poured coffee into big tin cups.

"This is all?" asked Uncle Fritz.

"That's trail rations until we hit buffalo country."

He didn't look happy, but he found something else to argue over. "Where is the plate and fork?"

"We travel light."

"So too the army, but the army has tin plates."

It was on my tongue to tell him if he was so partial to tin plates he should have joined the army, but likely that would bring on another law-and-order sermon. I speared a slab of salt pork with my knife and dropped it on a cut biscuit. After a moment, he did the same.

When we finished eating he wouldn't stand for me scraping the pans clean. I had to traipse down to the creek and wash them. I made him come along and entertained him with some of Possible's bloodiest Indian stories. He couldn't know Indians this side of Council Grove hadn't the gumption to do more than steal anything not tied down. I figured on curing him right quick of washing up after dark, but from the slow, thorough way he scrubbed out his skillet, I wasn't making much headway.

We no sooner bedded down by the fire when the clouds really let go. I was for climbing in the wagon, but Uncle Fritz wouldn't have it. He claimed we'd damage the trade goods the way we dripped and squished. We crawled under the wagon, but the wheels were so high and the rain so slanted I nearly drowned before morning. Considerable mud and wheel grease got mixed with the rain before it spattered us and puddled around our soggy blankets, but we didn't discover that until daylight.

Uncle Fritz stared at the blankets and my head, turned bright crimson and cussed in German. Leastways I think he cussed. I didn't ask for a translation. I used a few words myself that wouldn't stand explaining when he spent half the morning cleaning mud and grease from our hair, blankets and clothes. With rain and mud holes ahead, we'd be dirty again inside an hour and nobody we met was likely to be any cleaner. It was beyond me why Uncle Fritz insisted on cleaning fit for prayer meeting. I found out when we passed Round Grove.

With the fire circles, cropped grass, and scattered trash, I hardly needed Possible's description of landmarks to spot the place. Uncle Fritz got all worked up when I pointed out the campsite. He'd pictured a hotel, livery stable and a barber. He couldn't believe we could travel so far without reaching a town. I gave up trying to explain there was nothing between us and California. He'd see for himself. The only civilization we'd reach before Santa Fé was Bent's Fort, and if Uncle Fritz hadn't liked Independence he sure wouldn't cut any didoes over a trading post.

The sun broke through early in the afternoon, but we still spent more time pushing than riding. Uncle Fritz held down his side of the seat between mudholes, not talking. We didn't spot so much as a rabbit all day. When we pulled off to camp for the night, he led the team away without saying a word. While supper cooked, he studied the harness and stretched it full length across the bent grass. He was still studying and mumbling when supper was ready. I walked over to see what he was up to.

"Stand here." Uncle Fritz put me in front of the wagon, stepped over the harness and turned to face me. "Tomorrow we do all by order. You have one mule. I have one mule. *Eins,* we lift." He raised the foot-wide harness strap. "*Zwei,* over we throw. *Drei,* we pull tight."

He went on, numbering every harnessing motion until I smelled the biscuits.

"Very good," I told him. "But let's eat before everything burns."

Next morning we hitched according to Uncle Fritz's number system. It worked right well with the mules that were inclined to cooperate. Most of them weren't. We did get an earlier start, mostly because Uncle Fritz settled for a clothes brushing after breakfast instead of a thorough cleaning. At the rate we were not going, we fell short of every regular nooning ground and campsite. In a way I was glad. I wasn't anxious to make a laughingstock of ourselves standing like soldiers on either side of a pair of mules while Uncle Fritz barked, "*Eins, zwei, drei.*"

Uncle Fritz asked to drive, saying the orderly way to travel was to take turns. At first we hit more mudholes than ever, but he caught on faster than I had. Whoever drove cooked. The other tended the mules at rest stops and evening. Uncle Fritz dug out some paper and folded it into cups so he could measure the makings. That way his biscuits always came out the same, not bad but nothing to brag on either. I measured by guess and by golly. Some meals my biscuits were pretty sorry, but wondering how they'd turn out got to be the only interesting thing about our meals.

We both learned to spot the worst holes and bogs in time to turn the mules, but there were still places where Uncle Fritz had to muddy his frock coat and boots pushing the back wheel. We were lucky to be under-loaded and overteamed. If we'd carried a full load or taken only six mules, we'd have had to sit helpless until someone came along.

Early the fourth day we reached the Narrows, a treacherous strip of land between the Osage and Kansas rivers. Uncle Fritz was driving. The ground looked smooth and dry as a plank, but there was a blue-topped Conestoga painted OREGON FOR US mired hub deep.

"You'd better stop," I said. Possible had warned me about the Narrows.

"*Ja.*" But he let the mules plod on.

It took a spell for me to realize he thought I'd meant he should stop at the wagon. By that time the three youngsters chasing around the Conestoga spotted us. Their folks stopped digging at the wheels and the man ran toward us. Uncle Fritz pulled up when we met.

"Am I glad to see you," said the man. "We got left behind yesterday on account of a loose wheel. If you'll double team on my wagon, I'll do the same for you."

Uncle Fritz nodded. "First the wagon I take to the river. The team I bring back."

He cracked the whip and shouted, "Yaah! *Raus!*" The mules strained at the harness.

"Wait," called the Oregoner.

"We cross," said Uncle Fritz. The wagon rolled forward.

"You can't!"

But it was too late. Our wagon was already deep as the Conestoga and still sinking.

5

Orders from General Kearney

Double teaming the Conestoga's oxen with our mules was bad as tying dogs and cats together by the tails. We spent all day getting both wagons across the river onto solid ground. When we washed off the caked mud I hadn't one hand span of skin that wasn't mule kicked or ox bruised. I was for turning back right then, except it would mean crossing the Narrows again in the morning. One good thing, I missed Uncle Fritz's middling biscuits.

While we fought our wagon through the quagmire, the Oregoner's wife cooked up a pot of stew and baked two dried-apple pies. After supper the world looked brighter even if I did ache enough for twins. I lounged back on my blankets, listening to the emigrant brag on the farm he'd sold in Pennsylvania.

"It was poor, this farm?" asked Uncle Fritz.

The Oregoner bristled. "I should say not. My farm was the best in the county."

"Quincy tells me in Oregon there is nothing. Yet you sell your farm, a good farm by a law-filled city. Now you go to nothing. Why is that?"

"To keep the Britishers out, that's why. Oregon is ours. If enough of us get up there, the British will soon know it."

"The British claim—"

"They can claim all they want," the emigrant interrupted. "Who went to Oregon and fought the Indians? Who cleared the land and who owns it? Americans, that's who. It's ours, by God!"

"In Pennsylvania there are Germans?"

The Oregoner nodded. "Lots of them."

"Maybe someday they say, This is the Fatherland. We own it. Now it is German."

"They wouldn't dare!"

Uncle Fritz shrugged. "*Wurst wider Wurst.* You do it, they do it."

"They better not try. This is our country and we'll stomp anyone who says different."

He rose, tossed his coffee dregs into the fire and stalked off to his wagon. When we woke in the morning he was yoking the oxen. We started the fire, but the Oregoners didn't wait for breakfast, just pulled out without so much as a fare-thee-well.

"Dimwits and dunderheads," muttered Uncle Fritz. "Leaving good farms, good cities, and going to nothing."

"You did it," I reminded him.

"Did I know? Who tells me a city is no streets, no police, no order? Who tells me I will come with dunderhead mules to push a wagon?"

I threw skillets and pot into the wagon, doused the fire and ran for the team. Every step hurt from heel to neck, but I had to get Uncle Fritz's mind onto *eins, zwei, drei* before he worked himself into a case of apoplexy.

After a few days the rain petered out. We got the hang of wagon travel, but we never did catch up on the time we'd lost the first three days. It was late the eighth day instead of early the sixth when our wagon rolled down the slope to Council Grove Creek, 150 miles west of Independence. A strip of timber half a mile wide bordered the creek. Those oak, walnut, and hickory leaves did more for my sun-bleared eyes than ten hours' sleep.

Better than two hundred wagons were camped in bunches up and down the valley. The noise and confusion beat Independence six ways to Sunday. Hundreds of mules, horses and oxen pastured along the creek. Animal smells and wood smoke lay thick over the camps. I guided our wagon through with considerable more skill than I'd shown leaving Independence. Most clear places had maggoty belongings spread out to dry. If anyone dressed us down for running over them, it was lost in the general commotion.

"All these go to Oregon?" asked Uncle Fritz.

"Some of them. Others are heading for California. This is the last stretch of big timber, so they lay over to cut spare axles and form into trains." I spotted oversized high-wheeled wagons off to the far edge of the timber. "The traders are camped yonder."

When we pulled up at the traders' camp I was near bursting to find out if any of the wagons belonged to Cy Petry. But Uncle Fritz wouldn't let me go look until the mules were watered, fed, and staked. I spread the blankets, built a fire, and set the coffee pot to boil. Danged if Uncle Fritz didn't go around after me squaring the blanket edges and laying out the harness neat as a set of barber's tools. Then I fidgeted while he slicked himself fit for a wedding. His high hat was water spotted and the brim no longer curled up at the sides. The rest of his clothes had worn as poorly, but when he finally led the way to the center of traders' camp, he looked elegant next to the teamsters.

The traders were clustered around a wagon. A short bandy-legged man stood on the seat, waving his arms and spouting sixteen words to the dozen. From the sound of his voice he'd been at it quite a spell. Before he wound up and swung to the ground I understood he was aiming to be elected captain of the train. The next man to climb on the seat would have gotten my vote, if I'd had one. It was Cy Petry. His speech was so short I didn't have time to find Possible in the crowd.

"I been over this trail seven years straight," Cy told them. "I got more wagons than any of the rest of you, so I got more to lose if something goes wrong. Only I'll see that it don't. Come Indians, drought or Mexicans, I'm getting my men and wagons to Santa Fé. Elect me captain and I'll take you with me. All the way."

After some talk among themselves the wagon owners

lined up in front of the three men running for captain. Cy Petry's line was twice as long as either of the others.

The voting emptied most of the space around us. Possible and I spotted each other about the same time. After we'd whooped and thumped each other's back, I asked how come Cy was still camped in Council Grove.

"We're waiting on the prairie to dry. Nobody's getting through. Wagons been sending back for help with everything from broken axles to spoilt rations. I tell you, hoss, the only country I ever seen this wet was lake bottom."

"The sky's been clear the last three days," I said. "Maybe the bad weather's over."

"It's possible, but I wouldn't put beaver on it. I never knowed it to rain this far into June. No telling what that comet's fixing to do next."

Before I could express my views on the comet, Cy Petry climbed back to the wagon seat and cracked a whip for attention.

"All right, here's the rules. You do your own hunting, arrange your own messes and tend your own stock. When on the trail you can throw your loose stock in with mine and take turns herding if you've got men on horseback. Everyone fit to walk stands guard, one watch every other night. I'll appoint the sergeants of the guard soon as you line up and give me the number of your wagons and the names of your men."

Uncle Fritz and I tagged onto the end of the line. By the time we'd worked our way up, Cy had totaled thirty-eight wagons. I guessed the value of the train at close to $100,000 plus several hundred head of stock. With our half load of scraps and cuckoo clocks, I was almost ashamed to ask for a place in the train.

"Don't worry about it," Cy said. "We got more greenhorns now than the first years of the Santa Fé trade. Everyone with four wheels and a packet of pins is out to make a fortune."

He eyed Uncle Fritz's broad shoulders. "Sure glad to have you with us. Take the end of the shortest line when we pull out. As last comer you'll have to work your way up through the dust."

Uncle Fritz bowed stiffly. He was closer to grinning than I'd ever seen him. His look of satisfaction at Cy's law and order didn't last long. Two teamsters took exception to Cy's choice of guard sergeants. They dressed the new captain down with names hot enough to singe and threatened to unelect him on the spot. Uncle Fritz's cheeks flushed and I dragged him away before he began sermonizing and unjoined us from the train.

The next day Possible helped us check over the wagon, grease wheels, strengthen worn harness and swap bacon for two spare axles that we slung under the wagon. There was no time to cut and trim our own. Cy planned on leaving the next morning.

False dawn lit only the sky's edge when "Turn out! Turn out for Santa Fé!" wakened us, and I learned one reason we hadn't made good time from Independence: we'd eaten breakfast. Cy barely gave us time to roll and stow our blankets before "Catch up! Catch up!" went round the camp. Animals snorted and reared. Men cussed and harness jingled. Only one or two had time to gawk when Uncle Fritz started his count. I thought better of his *eins, zwei, drei* when I discovered we weren't the last to yell "All set!"

"Stretch out," Cy ordered.

The call went round the wagons followed by "Hep! Haw! Move out!" Whips cracked, and harness bells jingled.

"*Raus!*" Uncle Fritz paired the command with a satisfying crack of the whip. The wagon creaked, rocked, then lurched forward. Before full dawn, four lines of wagons straggled over the prairie, the loose stock herded off to one side. I wished I had a horse to explore the country, though there was never anything over the next grassy swell but another stretch of grass. Breakfast came at the first team rest, something so orderly and time-saving it surprised me that Uncle Fritz hadn't thought of it. But no, since he'd always breakfasted before traveling, he'd consider that the orderly thing to do.

We had a trouble-free day with weather a bit too fair for my liking. In spite of the grass and recent rain, dust from nine wagons plastered on me with sweat. Diamond Spring's gushing water set the whole train hoorahing.

Possible had thrown his rations in with ours, promised us a share of the game he shot for Cy's men, and elected me mess cook. Soon as the four lines of wagons became four sides of a square, I built a fire and ground coffee beans.

"Why are these wagon walls?" asked Uncle Fritz when he came from tending the mules.

"It's protection against Indian attacks," I told him.

"Why then are we outside?"

Possible strolled up to the fire with antelope steaks. "You're welcome to spread your blankets inside providing you don't take offense if a horse tromps you."

"No horses are in there."

"The saddle horses will be run in after they graze. So will all the stock on a bad night or if Injuns stalk us."

"And out here we stay with the Indians? Is the dimwitted mule better than a man?"

"It's possible. Can you pull a wagon?" The trapper held out his tin cup. "Fill up, Quince."

It wasn't one of my good biscuit nights, but with fresh meat, nobody seemed to mind. Cy came by to give guard assignments, adding that anyone caught sleeping or off his post would walk all the next day. Uncle Fritz nodded approval, but he refused to let me instruct him on loading and firing a rifle.

"Load one and leave it in the wagon," he said. "I need only to fire it once in warning."

Then he rolled up in his blankets until called for third watch. It was the first night I'd gone to bed easy in mind. With Cy Petry in charge and Possible to hunt for us, what could trouble us further? I found out next morning right after the order to catch up.

Half the camp was on hand to watch Uncle Fritz and me harness up. Possible joined the audience, but he just rubbed his hand high on his beard as if hiding a grin. The others called all sorts of funnies.

"Hey, Dutchie, when you going to teach them to read?" or "Watch out. Afore you know it, them mules will be smarter than you."

The morning was chill and frosty but my face

burned. I *eins-zwei*-ed fast as I could. For the first time those goll danged mules stood head high and tail still, as if pleased at the attention. It wasn't natural. I figured to be kicked any minute, but they didn't so much as shiver off a blowfly. By the time Uncle Fritz called "All is placed," the men had stopped catcalling.

"It do beat all," said one as they turned away. "Nobody catches up that fast lessen the prairie's on fire."

"Ever see mules stand like that?" wondered another. "He must have them witched."

I grinned as our side of the square pulled out. The wagon that had led the day before swung in behind us. We were working our way up, all right. The warm feeling I'd had the night before returned, but it didn't roost long.

Off to the northwest were boiling sulphur-yellow clouds with gray streaks trailing from them. The tall grass bent only where the wagons passed. No whips popped. No teamster cussed or grumbled. Every eye was gauging the storm. First it seemed as though it would pass behind us, but the cloud shadow moved faster than our wagons. We'd catch a wide strip of whatever devil's work was brewing.

Cy galloped past yelling, "Fort up! Fort up and hold your lead teams."

Everyone on horseback rode to drive the loose stock into the wagon square. In the queer yellow light the tangle of men and rearing animals reminded me of the hellfire and brimstone scenes circuit preachers always scared me with. Then way off the prairie stirred. The tall grass bent as the wind came at us. Lightning ripped so close I could smell sulphur.

The mules reared, nipped, and made enough racket to drown the thunder. I hung on to the right leader, shouting myself hoarse with a lullaby Mama used to sing. It was all I could think of, but it didn't comfort me or the mule. With a roar like the Missouri in flash flood, hailstones big as marbles beat down on us.

The mule quit fighting. I huddled against its quivering shoulder, teeth chattering and numb fingers gripping the harness. Ice balls hammered my back. Gales shook the wagons till I expected every one of them to sail back to Independence. Then, sudden as it had come, the storm passed and was gone.

The grass lay flat under uneven white ice. Where the sun's rays struck, only a narrow squint made the glare bearable. I pried my fingers loose from the harness and climbed back onto the wet seat.

Outside of ice cuts and bruises, the only loss was Uncle Fritz's hat, blown off in the first gust. The bandy-legged trader who'd run against Cy in the elections sold Uncle Fritz a wool felt hat with a wide floppy brim. He charged Santa Fé prices. I thought it was out-and-out thievery, but Uncle Fritz said it was just. A trader must make a profit, but I still thought the runt took advantage.

By the time we reformed our lines the ice had melted to large patches. Four hours later the sun had brought out midges and mosquitoes to plague us when we cut grass and willows to bridge muddy streams. What couldn't be bridged had to be forded with most everyone bogging down at least once. Two days of back-breaking misery got us to Cottonwood Creek, where the mud banks were so steep and high the wagons had to be led down and hauled up with ropes.

Uncle Fritz took a hand with the brace ropes. I agreed to drive. Double teamed, with brakes locked, the wagon tilted over the edge of the bank. Seconds later I was standing nearly upright on the footboard. The wagon swayed and all that kept me from jumping was Uncle Fritz counting away as the taut ropes drew the wagon upright, then slackened on Uncle Fritz's command. The rope team on the other side of the wagon didn't bother with *eins-zwei* or anything else. They just jerked and yanked, nearly dumping me into the stream. The worst part was going up the far bank. I could see the steep pitch and thought any minute I'd have sixteen mules falling backward on me. Afterwards, my knees shook so that I could hardly unhitch the teams.

There were still eight wagons to cross when the cry of "Buffalo!" went round the camp. Ropes dropped. Teams and wagons were forgotten in the rush to catch a saddled horse. I grabbed my gun from the wagon and ran after the riders. From the top of a rise I saw the herd. The near edge was a mile off. Beyond that, far as I could see, the prairie was a dark rolling mass of buffalo. With a whoop I trotted toward them. Horse or no horse, I wasn't passing up a chance to shoot a real live buffalo.

An hour later I crouched behind the carcass of a cow Possible had brought down and was butchering. The horsemen had ridden out of sight, shooting and yelling.

The herd was so big the hunters had only roiled it along the edge. I fired into the smelly, shaggy animals as they moved past. At that range I couldn't hardly miss. But outside of a kick and a quick sprint, the bullets had no more effect than a bee sting.

After a while Possible said, "You put enough lead into that shoulder hair, could be the weight will drag one to a stop and you can wait around till it starves to death."

That only made me more determined.

"You got to hit one spot just back of the shoulder if you want to drop a buffler." Possible tied the last of the choice meat onto the pack mules. "You coming, Quince?"

"No!"

"This herd will still be passing tomorrow."

"I might not get out tomorrow."

"Suit yourself, but it's a waste of lead and powder the way you're going at it."

He was right, but I stayed by the carcass long after he left, trying to prove him wrong. When I finally gave up and trudged back toward camp, the riders who caught up with me were just as shamefaced. They'd run their horses, risked their necks, and brought down no meat.

The trip back took longer than I'd figured. The walk out to the herd had slicked my boot soles so I kept slipping back on the bent grass. It was as hard on the legs as breaking snowdrifts. No wonder everyone hated walking. Cy couldn't have picked a better punishment for slack guards.

It was near dark when I reached camp. Possible and

73

Uncle Fritz had strips of buffalo roasting on green sticks, but I didn't get more than a smell.

"It is time for first guard," said Uncle Fritz.

What with one thing and another, I hadn't put anything in my stomach since morning. "I'll eat first."

"First guard is at sundown. If you are not at your post, Captain Petry will make you walk tomorrow."

"Eating won't take long. Besides, I just saw Cy sitting down to supper. How will he know if I'm late?"

"I will tell him."

One look at Uncle Fritz's face and I knew he would. I'd had enough slick grass walking.

"Go," ordered Uncle Fritz.

And I went, not even taking time to reload the rifle until I'd reached my post. Far as I could see, I was the only fool on duty. I sat and fumed.

Maybe Uncle Fritz had been a comfort when I crossed with the wagon. Maybe I was wrong to go off and leave Cy short-handed for the last wagons. But I wasn't the only green trader who'd caught buffalo fever and it was an unnatural uncle who'd report his own kin for taking the time to eat. After all, there was no law saying I had to stay with the train or obey Cy's rules. It was a free country. Uncle Fritz had no call threatening to report me to Cy.

My stomach rumbled so bad I couldn't have heard an Indian if he'd ridden up blowing a bugle. I figured on starving till morning, but when the second watch relieved me, I found a fresh pan of middling biscuits and plenty of meat sticks over the fire. Uncle Fritz must have heard me, but his blankets never stirred. That was all right by me. Any thanks I owed him for the meal would have stuck in my throat. No matter what, I'd never forget Mama's sweet baby brother had threatened to report me.

Due to buffalo crossing and several broken wagons, Cy ordered a layover next day. Uncle Fritz ordered baths and laundry.

"No law, no order," he grumbled as we dipped clothes in the creek. "Everything is what it should not be. Wagons sink in dry land. Ice freezes in summer. A backways country and the people are the same. Always they play when there is work."

"It's a free country," I told him. "If some folks want to hunt buffalo instead of scrubbing clothes, that's their right."

"Hunt! It is Possible has told me how they hunt. The dunderheads should do the work and leave hunting to hunters."

Deep down I knew he was right. Only experienced hunters could run buffalo, but his threat the night before still rankled. I was spoiling to tell Uncle Fritz what I thought of traitors, especially traitors who were kin. I'd have let loose right then if the Grand Army of the West hadn't showed up on the far bank.

Leastways I thought it was the Grand Army. Turned out it was only Captain Moore with two companies of the First Dragoons from Fort Leavenworth. They were hot on the trail of Armijo's wagons, the ones carrying Pa's gunpowder. Captain Moore stopped only long enough to pass on General Kearny's orders.

No wagon trains were allowed to go on to Santa Fé.

75

All were to wait at Pawnee Fork for an escort from the Grand Army of the West. After Bent's Fort they would proceed to Santa Fé with the army, under General Kearny's command. With news like that I could afford to forgive Uncle Fritz. Almost.

Cy ranted and fumed, but there wasn't a thing he could do but obey General Kearny's orders, not with two companies of dragoons to turn him back if he tried to sneak down the trail. Next day we headed for Pawnee Fork.

After Cottonwood Creek the only fuel was dried buffalo chips. They burned so fast it kept Uncle Fritz and me both scrambling to find enough. The land turned more desert than prairie. Cactus grew in patches, alkali dust burned our faces and hands, but there was water of sorts, mostly muddy and stinking from buffalo.

The rattlers held camp meeting over that whole section. I had the devil's own time keeping Uncle Fritz from being bit. Everybody knew rattlers were deadly poison. Everybody but Uncle Fritz. He'd never heard of a rattlesnake and for a while I didn't think he'd believe in them unless one bit him. Possible handed out advice on curing snake bite, including burning the wound with a red-hot iron. After that Uncle Fritz did his snake watching from a safe distance.

We celebrated Fourth of July on the trail. Every so often someone shot off a gun or started up a chorus of "Yankee Doodle." Uncle Fritz thought they were celebrating the coming rest at Pawnee Fork and Possible agreed not to tell him different. We might have skinned

76

through the day if Cy Petry hadn't decided the war obliged him to toast the country, the army and General Kearny. He broke out the snake-bite whiskey and brought it around to the cook fires after supper. Stubby Bowers, the skinflint who'd overcharged Uncle Fritz for the hat, was with him.

The jug made a couple rounds of our fire with Uncle Fritz and Possible seeing to it that I never held it long enough for even a sniff. While I was figuring a way to outmaneuver them Cy proceeded to explain Independence Day to Uncle Fritz.

Uncle Fritz was already so flushed from heat and whiskey there was no telling how riled he was getting. I prayed neither Cy nor Stubby Bowers got fighting mean on whiskey. Then again, I wouldn't mind seeing Uncle Fritz taken down a peg. Any man who threatened to report his blood kin deserved it. Only Pa would skin me alive if I stood by and let Mama's baby brother take a whomping.

I scrooched backwards till I was in the shadows. Then I got to my feet, edged to the rear of our wagon and drew out my rifle. I hadn't acted any too soon. Cy was taking the jug away from Stubby Bowers and Uncle Fritz was rising to speak his piece on independence.

6

A
Dunderhead Army

"Is it not bad enough you fought against your lawful ruler?" said Uncle Fritz. "Must you celebrate your lawlessness each year? But one should expect this in such a country."

Stubby Bowers shook his fat finger at Uncle Fritz. "This is an almighty fine country and you can't say otherwise."

His words were slurred, and from the way Cy frowned at him and hefted the jug, Stubby overdrank as heavily as he overcharged.

"No, sir," he repeated. "You can't say otherwise."

But Uncle Fritz did. "This is a country without laws. Men fight in the streets with no one to stop them. There are thieves and they are never caught. When there is work to do, the men run off to shoot."

"I'll drink to that last one," said Cy.

Stubby turned on him. "Yeah? Try this Dutchie's

78

eins-zwei on us and we'll have ourselves a new captain."

"You fixing to run again?" Cy and Stubby were on their feet, glaring at each other.

"It's a free country," said Stubby.

"*Ja,*" boomed Uncle Fritz. "Free for thieves and dunderheads."

Stubby hunched down like a heavy bulldog about to take on a bear. "You watch out, Dutchie. Maybe we don't *eins-zwei* every time we pull our trousers on, but we get things done. We're likely to do something about you if you don't keep that tater trap shut."

"It's a free country," I said, stepping up behind Uncle Fritz. I didn't aim the rifle, just carried it ready over my left elbow.

Cy grinned, took the jug in one hand and Stubby's arm in the other. "You sure told him proper, Stubby."

"About time, too. *Eins-zwei*-ing everybody deef and dumb," Stubby complained.

We could hear Cy agreeing as he led the swaying trader around the line of wagons.

"You always hunt rabbit with a cannon?" Possible asked me.

Uncle Fritz turned and looked down at the gun. "It is not your night for guard duty, Quince."

I hadn't felt so foolish since the night Will had sent Les and me on a wild chase for a bird so rare it didn't exist. Cy hadn't needed any help. I might even have made things worse bringing a gun into the argument. All I could think of to get out of the spot was to hand the rifle to Uncle Fritz.

79

"You have second shift tonight," I said.

"I will take it when it is time. Put it away."

"Tell you what, Eins-Zwei," said Possible. "When we lay over in Pawnee Fork I'll learn you to load that thing and hit something."

Uncle Fritz shook his head. "Guns I leave to soldiers and hunters. I do not need them."

"That's possible, but we'll be traveling with the army afore long."

"I am a clockmaker, not a soldier. I guard only because it is Captain Petry's order."

When we settled at Pawnee Fork he dug out his clockmaker's box with knives, hooks, and tiny gadgets in velvet-lined sections. Then he took out the broken clock he'd carted all the way from Independence and set to work carving new wheels and gears.

Santa Fé trains rolled in almost daily. There were better than two hundred wagons when Captain Moore returned with his dragoons. He hadn't caught Armijo, but he led us on to Bent's Fort to await the rendezvous of the Grand Army.

All along the Arkansas River the wagons wound through high glaring sand hills. As the trail climbed, the sand hills fell away. A week after leaving Pawnee Fork we rolled out on the edge of a great plain.

Possible rode up beside our wagon. "Well, hoss, what do you see?"

"Nothing. Hundreds and hundreds of miles of nothing."

"God be with us," Uncle Fritz murmured in German.

After Possible pointed them out I could see the dark

clouds ahead on the horizon were really mountains.

"The Great Rockies," said Possible. "Those two humpy shadows to the southwest are Spanish Peaks. You'll get a closer look at them."

Then he pointed to the northwest. "That shiny peak under the clouds is Pike's Peak, still snow-topped."

I shaded my eyes and gazed at the mountain I'd dreamed of back in Pa's store. "I've come a far piece from Independence, that's for sure." And so far the trip wasn't at all what I'd expected.

"That you have, Quince. And you're going a lot farther."

"God help us," Uncle Fritz said again.

I couldn't help grinning at the way he'd argued when I'd told him there were no inns or barber shops for more than a thousand miles. With his thick beard and floppy brimmed hat, Pa would never know him. Not unless Uncle Fritz bumped against disorder. Inside, old Eins-Zwei hadn't changed a bit.

Early in the afternoon we caught our first glimpse of Bent's Fort. The high log walls looked more like a military stockade than a trading post. Maybe the Indians camped around the fort weren't always peaceful.

Captain Moore camped us two miles below the fort. I didn't get a footstep closer till I'd helped Uncle Fritz pull the wagon wheels off one by one to soak them overnight in the river. They'd dried out so bad they rattled and we'd lost a few spokes. Following Possible's advice, we soaked them tight. When they'd been replaced and greased, the wagon and harness checked inch by inch and repaired, Uncle Fritz settled down to his whittling. After three days of itching I could finally stroll over to the fort and gawk at the Indians.

They looked nothing like the ones around Independence. For one thing, they stared right back till I felt like crawling in the nearest hole and pulling it shut after me. I didn't venture into their camps without Possible at my side.

He warned me against lice-filled buffalo robes, but I wanted to take something back to Independence that would prove I'd met wild Indians. I favored a couple of arrows. Then I could say offhand, "Got this from a wild Indian on the plains, but I made a fair trade for it." If someone like Sue Ellen Hodges took it to mean I'd been in an Indian fight, so much the better. But Possible argued me into trading for a pair of moccasins.

He parleyed with a stout squaw until she agreed to make two pairs, one for me and one for Uncle Fritz, in exchange for one of our larger looking-glasses. She outlined my bare feet on a piece of thick dirty hide that Possible said was a piece of her old tepee. I regretted not sticking to arrows, but when she came to our wagon for Uncle Fritz's footprints, she brought me a pair of moccasins I wouldn't have traded for a quiverful of arrows.

Only the soles were of the thick hide. The tops were soft leather worked with bright beads.

"Trade beads," Possible said disgustedly when he saw them. "They should be dried quills."

But I was proud as a jay. Uncle Fritz looked grimmer than ever when he chanced to look at my feet.

He packed his pair away and tried hard to ignore mine.

I didn't give up on the arrow, though. If I found one around the camps I could still say something like, "I picked this up on the prairie. It was shot by a wild Indian." Which would be the truth, far as it went. I took to circling around the fort and camps but without any luck. Then, the end of July, the Grand Army of the West arrived.

We could see them spread for miles over the plain, sidling off from bunches to shoot at jack rabbits. From the way they moseyed along scattered all over the country, the army would be a full day or more reaching Bent's Fort. After a half-hour Uncle Fritz refused to watch the growing specks. About noon the first groups rode close enough for us to cheer them toward their camps. After that most everyone lost interest. I got discouraged myself. With eight hundred men straggling in from all directions to a dozen different campsites, I hadn't much chance of greeting Will and Les. Best thing was to wait until they were all in and settled.

Just before dusk I started supper, then went to invite Will and Les to share it. Possible wouldn't be eating with us. He'd discovered Fitzpatrick was scouting for General Kearny and had gone to spend the night with his old trapping crony.

After asking at several camps I found out the Independence volunteers had been given well-digging duty. I stumbled through the stickery river brush to a spot of light. Three men stood watching a fourth man dig. One of them held a lantern over the hole. Right off, I had to explain what I was doing more than five hundred miles from Independence. They didn't know where Les and Will were digging, but Joe Murphy told me they'd be together since they shared the same tent. Work details usually went to messmates.

The next three I met had struck water and were going back to camp. One told me he'd seen Will headed downriver just a short time before. By the time I reached the next well it was full dark. All I could see were two dark shapes against the lantern light. First off I thought I'd made a mistake. They both carried rifles as if on guard, but they looked down at a fresh-dug hole. I crept to within a few yards before I was certain they were Will and Les.

"Water isn't so scarce you have to guard it," I called.

"Who's that?" Les said as they turned.

Their jaws dropped and they stared in disbelief. Then they were on me, wrestling and whooping, demanding to know if I'd run off from home to join the army. Right in the middle of my explaining, a muddy volunteer climbed out of the hole.

A raspy voice said, "You stinking cowards trying to drown me?"

If Will and Les had gone slack-jawed at seeing me, it was nothing to the way I must have looked coming face to face with Rufus Purdy.

"Well, if it ain't my old friend Quincy," said Rufus. "You put them up to drowning me?"

"Nobody tried to drown you," Will said.

"I yelled twice for help. The stinking water was up to my knees."

His trousers didn't look wet, though it was hard to be

sure in such poor light. Rufus kept eyeing me, as if wondering who'd come with me and why. For my own safety I'd have let him worry, but Les told him about Uncle Fritz and Cy Petry's wagon train. At his first stop for breath I cut in.

"Possible left us plenty of antelope steaks for supper if you'd care to join us."

Rufus just naturally figured he was included. Will thought so too, for when Rufus stepped around the well to fetch his rifle, Will whispered, "Thanks, Quince. This will get him off our necks for holding a gun on him. It was the only way we could get him to do his share of the digging."

Rufus fell into step beside us. Les called to Hank Fletcher that the well was filling and they were off to the traders' camp. As we passed between the wagons Rufus hung back to inspect them. I hated to think why, but it gave the chance I'd waited for.

"What's he doing here?" I asked.

Les stared at me. "Why, Rufus joined up. Don't you remember? You had everyone looking for him the night before we left. You said then he'd volunteered."

"That was his story. He helped Armijo rob Pa's store."

"He couldn't have, Quince. He was out chasing his horse."

"He swore to it, Quince." Will's tone was mocking. "So we all just naturally have to believe it."

"He tracked that horse most all night," Les went on. "By the time he caught up with it, he was so far out of town that he just made camp. He joined up with us two days out of Independence."

"And we've met his sunny face and cheerful disposition every morning since," said Will. "Good old Les invited honest Injun Purdy to share our tent. Nobody else would have him."

"I'm the only friend Rufus got," Les said.

"You're the only person fool enough to believe everything he tells you." Will's voice had lost its usual half chuckle. "The Purdys are the biggest thieves west of the Mississippi."

"Now, Will, you got no call running Rufus down just because he was born a Purdy. He couldn't help that."

"He doesn't have to live like one," I put in. "You forget who stole your pa's calf last summer?"

"His uncle made him," Les said. "Rufus told me. He's right sorry about it, too."

I snorted. "Most likely his uncle didn't share."

Will put his arm over Les's shoulder. "Forgive us, Brother Les, if we cannot share your struggle to redeem the sinner. Labor onward if you must. And when Brother Rufus backslides, don't despair. The devil takes care of his own."

"Now, Will . . ."

I glanced past Les's shoulder. Rufus was catching up with us. I shushed Les and we swapped travel stories until we reached our wagon. I wondered if Rufus recognized it as the one left in our alley but I couldn't watch him and Uncle Fritz both. They'd all met in Independence but that seemed so long ago I introduced them all over again.

Uncle Fritz didn't honor any of them with a bow, but he at least kept his opinions of the Grand Army to himself. He'd finished the cooking. I poured coffee while the three volunteers dug into the food. It was the first fresh meat they'd had since leaving Fort Leavenworth.

"In this stinking army all you get is breakfast," complained Rufus.

"You're issued a full day's rations every morning." From the weariness in Will's voice it wasn't the first time he'd explained it to Rufus. "You're not supposed to cook everything for breakfast and then throw away what's left."

I didn't dare look at Uncle Fritz.

"Who's got any left to throw away?" asked Les.

"As for our attempts at hunting . . ." Will paused, then grinned at me. "If you joined, Quince, you'd be our top marksman."

I refused to believe Will wasn't overstretching the truth. Not with a war ahead of them.

"The army has to feed you proper, don't they?" I asked.

"They try." Will explained there were supply wagons and a herd of beef cattle, but with the army moving in stray bunches and the supply wagons dispatched at three-day intervals, wagons and men never seemed to meet. They'd been on half rations for the past week.

Uncle Fritz made a noise of disgust. "What can be expected from an army that does not give clothes to its soldiers?"

"We got clothes." But Les looked down at his stained coat and trousers as if to make sure.

87

"Armies must have uniforms. Uniforms must be brushed and the gold buttons polished."

Rufus speared another steak from the skillet. "This stinking army don't hand out uniforms."

"They allow us forty-two dollars for clothing," said Les.

"Allow ain't pay," Rufus told him. "They allow us forty dollars for our time, too, but what did they give us? Fifteen stinking dollars for our horses, that's what. And mine is worth every bit of thirty-four."

"Did you ask the price before you took it?" asked Will.

Rufus's eyes narrowed. "Just because I don't dig up unfinished business, don't think I've forgot. I got a long memory, Will Dayton, and today's give me something to add to it."

His whispery voice sent a chill up my spine. If Will felt anything, it didn't show. He went right into stories of the march from Fort Leavenworth. General Kearny had pushed them thirty or more miles a day. Surprisingly, the battalion of infantry made better time than the dragoons, and the way horses were dropping, Will feared they'd all end up infantry. Worst of the lot were the German volunteers from St. Louis. If they didn't get lost, their cannon bogged down. It was plain they were the joke of the Grand Army.

All the time Will talked I kept sneaking glances at Rufus. Something about him dragged at my memory. While I worried at it, Hank Fletcher stepped into the firelight.

"Les," he said shortly. "You were due on guard duty twenty minutes ago."

"Aw, not tonight, Hank."

"*Lieutenant* Hank," Will corrected. "You must go with the officer and do your duty, Les, old soldier."

"Not tonight, I don't. I'm having a good time for a change. Besides, I come to fight for my country, not to march back and forth all night by my lonesome."

Uncle Fritz sounded as if something had caught in his windpipe.

"We'll see about that." Lt. Hank Fletcher turned on his heel and strode off.

"Stinking officers," muttered Rufus. "Next time we have an election, nobody over private's getting my vote."

Before I could stop them, Will and Les ran off the story of the elections at Fort Leavenworth. The volunteer officers had been elected the same as Cy Petry, only there'd been days of heavy campaigning at Fort Leavenworth. Alexander Doniphan had been elected colonel, mostly, claimed Will, because his home town had provided free breakfasts during the campaign.

Uncle Fritz burst into German. "What army ever elects their own officers? What army permits a soldier to refuse guard duty? This is an army of dunderheads led by imbeciles."

There was a lot more, but my German gave out.

"What ails him?" whispered Les.

"Dunderhead fever," I said, but only Will seemed to catch a hint of my meaning.

Uncle Fritz broke off when a deep voice called, "Les, could I have a word with you?"

A man big as Uncle Fritz stood in the shadows between the wagons. Les rose quickly and walked over. A few minutes later the man left quietly.

Les came back grinning sheepishly. "I got guard duty."

"I thought you didn't like walking back and forth by your lonesome," said Will.

"I don't, but the way Colonel Doniphan explained it I couldn't hardly refuse."

"Explained!" thundered Uncle Fritz.

"Stinking officers," muttered Rufus.

Les said, "See you tomorrow. Thanks for the supper."

When he picked up his rifle I knew what had bothered me about Rufus. His rifle. It reminded me of the one I'd dreamed over in Pa's store. The way Rufus had his rifle tucked under his thigh, I couldn't get a look at the stock until he rose to leave with Will. Even then I couldn't be certain of anything except there weren't any ivory buffalo heads reflecting the firelight.

Everything seemed to prove I'd wronged Rufus. Certainly everyone except Will seemed to think so. Maybe I'd dreamed his voice in the alley that night.

"It's possible," I muttered as I rolled into my blankets. "But I don't believe it. Leastways not until I get a good close look at that rifle stock."

How I was to manage that without giving Rufus a chance to settle old scores was something I hadn't figured out. The thought of Rufus Purdy in camp with a rifle was uncomfortable enough.

7

The Alkali Trail

The next morning I saw Will and Les only from a distance and Rufus Purdy not at all. General Kearny ordered two hours of morning drill for all volunteers, then a talk on the proper care of horses followed by an afternoon of more drilling.

The volunteers didn't take to all that military order. They stumbled through the commands as if they didn't know right from up, flopped down in the shade, dropped their sun-heated rifles and drove the regular officers into tempers much like Uncle Fritz's.

I watched, along with most of the wagoners, hooting and catcalling and having a good laugh at the volunteers' expense. Then I heard Stubby Bowers yell, "Don't let them *eins-zwei* you, boys. Sit down on your rights." It brought close the morning they'd made fun of Uncle Fritz and me. For a reason I couldn't tie down, the reminder made me uneasy.

Cy didn't help when he told Stubby, "Those boys may need a bit of the *eins-zwei* before they're done."

I turned away and wandered over beyond the fort to watch the prairie dogs and make a halfhearted search for an old arrow. I got back to the wagon in plenty of time to start supper, but Will and Les were there before me.

"Where's Rufus?" I asked. If anyone cadged a free meal, it would be him.

Will shook his head. "Haven't seen him since early morning."

I couldn't tell which bothered me most, hearing that raspy voice at my shoulder or not knowing where Rufus might be skulking.

"You'll stay for supper," I said.

"Your uncle already asked us."

Only hearing that Uncle Fritz had signed with the volunteers would have surprised me more. I went to the rear of the wagon where he was slicing meat.

"Thanks for asking them to supper," I whispered.

"They are only two," he said gruffly. "We cannot feed all the dunderhead army."

From the way he cut into our rations, it looked as if he planned to. Possible had gone with Fitzpatrick to scout the trail to Raton Pass, so we were back on salt pork, biscuits and the last of the stale broken crackers. While we ate, Will and Les bickered over the day's drilling. Surprisingly, Will was for it, especially the horse care lessons.

"Now, Will," Les said, "you know I don't need that. We had horses back home."

92

"The captain touched on a good many things you never run into with a plow team," Will argued. "Saddle sores, for instance. You looked at your horse's back lately?"

"That's heat rash."

Will rolled his eyes to the stars and shook his head.

"As for all that right, left, and about-face," Les continued, "we come to fight the Mexicans, not march them to death."

There was no denying he had a point.

Will gave up. "I'm too tired to argue. Let's go turn in. Reveille sounds at four-thirty, even in camp."

"Getting up that early is sillier than horse school," Les grumbled. "We got no cows to milk."

After he'd thanked Uncle Fritz for supper, Les told me, "I'll see you for sure tomorrow, Quince. When that captain calls drill, I'm not going to be in hearing distance. Let's you and me find a hidey hole down by the river."

Most of the volunteers must have made the same plan. Fewer than a third of them showed for drill next day. Will was one of them, but Les met me at the river after my morning chores were done. We sneaked way down below the fort and spent the day swimming, pitching rocks and bragging on all we'd been through since leaving Independence. The only thing about the army Les had a good word for was Rufus Purdy. While we lay on the stony bank, shaded from the hot afternoon sun, we got around to wondering which of the rumors going around camp was true.

Governor Armijo was said to be mustering two thousand Mexicans and Indians to defend Santa Fé. That was better than two to one against the volunteers. Another rumor had it that Armijo wouldn't fire a shot.

"It sure would be a disappointment to come all this ways for nothing," Les said.

He needn't have worried. Only someone planning to fight sent out spies, and when we returned to camp, everyone was all fired up about Mexican spies. Possible and Fitzpatrick, returning from their scout, had come on two Mexicans not far from where Les and I had been swimming. The spies carried letters addressed to General Kearny, which turned out to be blank paper but would have gotten them past our patrols. Only Rufus Purdy had captured them and Rufus, who couldn't read any better than Possible, hadn't paid any heed to the letters.

Leastways Rufus had been with the Mexicans when Possible and Fitzpatrick found them. Rufus claimed he'd captured them and everyone was giving him the credit.

Les all but turned handsprings at the news. "Will's been talking down on Rufus. He'll change his tune now."

"I'll see you at supper." I made tracks for our wagon, hoping to find Possible and get the rights of Rufus and his supposed capture of the Mexican spies.

Possible hunkered by our fire, drinking coffee and listening to Uncle Fritz explain why we'd lost the war before we'd rightly started.

"This governor of the laws and taxes," he said. "He

sends spies and prepares for war. What does this army of dunderheads? They swim and shoot at rabbits and sit in the shade."

If he could have worked a little worry into his voice I might have taken it that he was on our side. For Mama's sake I gave him the benefit of the doubt.

"We got spies of sorts," Possible said. "There's a Maguffin been living in Mexico a spell. He's taking his Yankee bride back to Santa Fé. Left the fort yesterday."

"Is he going to spy for General Kearny?" I asked.

"It's possible, but from what I hear, he aims to talk Armijo into breaking the war club afore we get there."

"Then we might not fight at all." It was kind of disappointing. I wanted some adventuring before seeing Independence again.

"Good," said Uncle Fritz. "A no fighting war is all this army can win."

"Whose side are you on?" I asked.

"No side. I make clocks." And he stomped off to tend the mules.

While he was gone I asked Possible if he thought Rufus had really planned on bringing the Mexicans in at gunpoint.

"What I think don't matter. Only what I saw."

"I never knew you to shy at giving an opinion." A terrible thought crossed my mind. "Uncle Fritz must be talking you over to his ways just like a preacher at revival."

"You could do worse than listen to Eins-Zwei."

"I've listened to him ever since he came."

95

The old trapper shook his head. "You hear, Quince, but you don't listen. Now I recollect one time old Chief Shinnydoor told—"

I interrupted before he caught me up in one of his yarns. "What about Rufus?"

"I can only tell you what I saw. Rufus was standing down in a washed-out river gully with those two Mexicans."

"Was he pointing his rifle at them?"

"Fitzpatrick says he was and I can't swear otherwise. But just a breath afore we reached the edge of the bank, I caught a flash of sun. If I'd been scouting a war party, I'd have said it glanced off a moving gun barrel."

"Then Rufus heard you coming and turned on the Mexicans to protect himself."

"It's possible, but I wouldn't go saying it around camp. Rufus Purdy's war chief right now."

The rest of his story was the same as I'd already heard. Rufus had claimed the capture of two spies. Fitzgerald and Possible had ridden alongside them to General Kearny's tent. If it hadn't been for the fight behind Pa's store, I might have believed it. While I tried to figure how much damage a traitor could do the Grand Army, Les showed up.

The supply wagons had arrived and cattle had been butchered. The volunteers were feasting and Les wanted us to join them. Possible begged off. He and Fitzgerald wanted to swap yarns. Uncle Fritz said he'd stay with them, if Possible didn't mind. He'd probably sermonize the trappers till their ears numbed.

When we reached the small patched tent Les shared

with Will and Rufus, I was sorry I'd accepted the invitation. All the Independence volunteers were gathered around hoorahing Rufus like he'd taken Santa Fé single-handed. Les acted foolish as the rest, but Will looked on with a mocking grin.

I joined the crowd long enough to be sure Rufus wasn't carrying his rifle. I couldn't ransack the tent, but the one good look I had inside proved the rifle could only be under the blankets. Why hide it unless Rufus feared to have me see it? Certainly Les must have told him I'd be here. I didn't stay long. When I got up to leave, Will came with me.

"Brother Purdy's done a good deed in spite of himself." Will's tone sobered as he glanced back at the whooping volunteers. "They needed something to celebrate tonight. One of the companies held a double funeral today."

"No! I'd heard measles were going around, but I didn't know it was that bad."

"There's fever as well and some are just worn out. More than twenty are being left at the fort. They're too sick to go on. Maybe too sick to return."

We walked slowly, not talking. When we reached the dark quiet between company camps, I stopped and told Will of the sun flash Possible had noticed.

"Quince, are you trying to prod me into saying that Rufus is working for the Mexicans?"

"It adds up, don't it?"

"Sure, but the answer depends on who's doing the figuring." His voice rose just long enough to override my protest. "Now hold on, Quince. I don't trust Rufus

97

any more than you do. I've been fast-stepping to keep him from catching me in a lonely corner."

"I don't know how you've held him off this long."

"Rufus doesn't like witnesses. He won't do anything with the army around. I think he took up with Les at Fort Leavenworth just on the off chance of catching me alone. I've had some near scrapes on work details." He was silent a moment, then said briskly, "As I was saying, there are two ways of figuring Brother Purdy. He could have found those two Mexicans the same time as Possible and Fitzpatrick. Possible could have seen the gun shine just as Rufus moved in."

"He could have been covering his double-dealing just as easy."

"Suppose you're right, Quince. What information could Rufus give that the spies couldn't already have seen for themselves from any high spot near camp?"

"None." On the face of it, Will was right. "I'll admit I'd be back there cheering with the rest if he hadn't helped the Mexicans rob Pa's store. Only I don't expect you believe that either."

"That's the one thing I know for sure."

"Why? Nobody else believes me."

"Nobody else helped you put Rufus out of the wagon. We're the only ones who'd be listening for that voice and make no mistake when we heard it. There's just one thing bothering me. Rufus could have hidden out in St. Louis or with the Indians. Why did he join the volunteers? He had nothing to gain."

"Armijo's brother must have paid him to join."

At last Will sounded worried. "It's the only answer

that makes sense, but what is Rufus supposed to do to earn the money? Armijo must already know as much about the Grand Army as we do."

"Maybe Rufus is supposed to do something and Armijo's keeping in touch until the time comes."

If that was true, the closer we got to Santa Fé, the more dangerous Rufus would become. And we had no proof to give the regular officers. Then I remembered the rifle.

"Will, did you ever notice any marks on Rufus's gun stock, as if something had been pried off?"

"I try to overlook Rufus. It isn't easy in the same tent."

When I'd explained my suspicions, Will agreed to inspect the rifle.

"But only if I can do it so Rufus won't know," he added. "I'm not ready for a bar-nothing fight with Rufus Purdy."

Neither was I. We ended up deciding the best we could do was keep close watch on Rufus in hopes we'd turn up something to give the officers before reaching Santa Fé.

Next morning General Kearny sent the two Mexican spies on a tour of the camp. If looks made a villain, these were two of the worst in creation. One had squinty nervous eyes and a broken nose. If the other thought his long greasy mustache prettied the scar across his cheek, he was mistaken. I'd hate to meet either of them in a dark alley. There was a good chance Uncle Fritz and I already had.

In the afternoon General Kearny set them free. Will

wasn't around to give me that smug, knowing grin. Part of the army, including the Independence volunteers, had moved nine miles below Bent's Fort to get a head start next morning. Possible said traveling in bunches would keep everyone from reaching water at the same time. I worried that I might not see Will again until the army rendezvoused at the Purgatoire.

Uncle Fritz looked almost cheerful at the order to move out next day. He'd carved all the gears and innards but claimed there was too much dust blowing in camp for him to risk unwrapping the broken clock. He wasn't the only one anxious to move on. Cy kept muttering that here it was the first of August and we should have reached Santa Fé. For the first time since Council Grove I went to bed eager for the morning call.

Only the mules were set on staying. They balked, fought and kicked as if they'd never felt a harness strap. Uncle Fritz calmly *eins-zwei*-ed, dodged a kick, and went on to *drei* as if the mule had never moved. I cussed, hauled and kicked back. So did everybody else. The camp looked like a battleground and some of the teamsters ended up as bloody as if it was. The army had begun moving out when we brought in the teams. By the time we'd caught up, even the supply wagons had gone.

A couple miles of honest work settled the team. By then my throat rasped and my arms ached clear down my spine. The dust didn't help. It carried alkali that burned the eyes and cracked the lips. Even the lead wagons couldn't escape it. The wind blew so hard it seemed the whole blamed country was emigrating.

We covered twenty miles that day and not a drop of water along the trail. What we carried in the two barrels went to the mules, save for a few skimpy swallows, and it wasn't enough. When the water hole came in sight at sundown, I dropped the reins, leaped to the ground and outran the team to wallow like a hog in a slough. The cavalry ahead of us had tromped the thick green scum to bits and mixed it with bottom mud, but to me that water tasted sweet as the icy fountain at Diamond Spring.

The cavalry had moved on, no one knew where. The German artillery from St. Louis was lost again and only the infantry camped near us. I didn't look for Will until I heard talk of a stampede the night before. The companies that had moved below the fort had lost over thirty horses. Their owners had been forced to join the infantry.

Tired as I was, I dragged through the infantry camp until I found Will and Les sprawled on the stony ground, boots and packs dropped any which way. Les raised up on an elbow at my greeting, but Will just lifted a hand and let it fall.

"We lost our horses." Les sounded as if I was somehow to blame.

"I heard. It's too bad." I dropped down between them. "Where's Rufus?"

"Looking for his horse, last I heard." Will's voice held only weariness. "I'm sure he'll find it."

"Rufus knows how to track, all right," Les said. "Maybe he'll find ours too."

"I wouldn't sit here and wait for him." Will turned

on his side to look at me. "Before you bust, Quince, I'll tell you. Rufus was on guard duty when the stampede started."

"Was he guarding the herd?"

"No, but he was closest of anyone in camp. I've asked around and nobody recalls seeing him at his post. Not that it proves he wasn't there. Most of us doze off on guard duty and only the regulars really walk the post."

Les glanced from Will to me, frowning with the effort to catch the drift of our talk.

"The Mexicans were released soon after you left yesterday," I told them.

"I know," Les said. "We saw them."

Will sat up. "When?"

"I don't recollect exactly. Just a while before we made camp. Rufus gave them some water."

I stared at Will. "Didn't you see them?"

He shook his head. "I had to stop a few times. I kept dropping back till I was one of the last in camp."

"Thirty horses should bring a nice price in Santa Fé," I said. "Even split three ways."

Will grinned weakly. "I'd sure hate to try collecting my share from those two."

"Rufus might could do it." Then I asked, "What started the stampede?"

"Nobody knows." Will lay back with a sigh and covered his eyes with his arm. "Nobody knows anything for sure, Quince, and at the rate we're going, nobody ever will."

"I sure won't if one of you doesn't tell me," Les burst out.

"Tomorrow," Will told him. "Right now I'm just as sore as too tired."

Before I took my leave I pulled Will's blanket from his pack and covered him. I tossed Les his and promised to see them at camp next night. Will looked sure enough sick, but I told myself it was just all that dry marching. He'd perk up when he was used to it.

We pulled out next day with barrels full of scummy water. We'd been told there was water thirteen miles ahead, but Possible warned us that a number of things could have happened to it since he and Fitzpatrick had scouted through. We found the water hole thick and churned as the one we'd left, with rotting snakes and a dead bloated horse added for flavor. The mules didn't mind, but Cy Petry decided we must follow the army clear to Hole in the Prairie.

The wagon jolted along hour after hour. Heat waves made the dwarf cedars shimmer so I couldn't see straight. We passed so many dead mules and horses that a half-mile stretch without them seemed unnatural. The wagons chased crows and wolves from the carcasses, but they just waited out of gunshot till we passed. The dead animals should have warned me, but the first grave shocked me like a swallowed lump of ice.

I turned as we passed and hung over the side until I could no longer see the long mound of rocks through the dust. It may have been an old grave, but the next we passed was marked by a cross of twigs and the rocks were fresh-piled. Uncle Fritz said nothing and the bit of face between beard and hat brim was so coated with alkali dust I'd have been hard put naming him in a crowd, let alone figuring what he was thinking.

I counted four graves. How many we passed after dark I don't know. By then I wasn't sure anymore where I was headed or why. The world was nothing but a spine-bruising wagon seat, bobbing mules' ears and the moonlit wagon ahead.

Three hours after full dark we reached Hole in the Prairie. I disremember how many buckets of water I hauled from the deep spring to water us and the mules and refill the barrels. Uncle Fritz did more than his share, working regular as one of his clocks, though he moved as if he'd soon need rewinding. While staggering through the chores I caught bits of talk about scouting Raton Pass for ambush, but I wasn't fit to pay much heed. My eyes burned and watered from the alkali. My lips were so sore I had to force food past them. Maybe Will and Les were better off in the infantry. There couldn't be much dust on foot. If both were still on their feet. I pushed that fear aside.

The next two days were more of the same except the wolves took to following the wagons. When we reached the Purgatoire, I stripped and threw myself into the swift, sweet river. Uncle Fritz drank until he got sick, but he wound himself up enough to help tend the mules. While we staked them out, Possible strolled up.

"We start up the pass tomorrow," he told Uncle Fritz. "Better check the wagon and harness."

Uncle Fritz's nod drained what little strength the water had given me. I would have soaked in that river till I was wrinkled as the last apple in the barrel except that I wanted to search for Will. Old Eins-Zwei wouldn't let me out of sight now until everything was greased, polished and mended. I followed him back toward the wagon, taking no notice of anything until my nose rammed against his barn-door back.

I tried to look around him. He moved to block my view but not before I'd seen the burial detail moving away from the army camp.

"Go ask your friends to supper," he said. "Later we will work."

I was gone long enough for him and Possible to lever up the wagon and replace a split axle. When I came back, Possible was putting on a wheel while Uncle Fritz greased the other three. They straightened and looked at me.

I shook my head. "They haven't come in yet."

"That don't mean nothing," Possible said. "Lots of stragglers don't come in till near midnight."

"They have been seen?" Uncle Fritz, too, must have been thinking of the graves we'd passed.

"Yes, but everyone's too bumfuzzled to remember just where or when."

When Possible stepped back from the wheel, Uncle Fritz greased it carefully with the mixture of tallow and pine pitch, set the cover square on the leather bucket and hung it in place under the wagon.

"After supper we mend the harness," he said, and went off to trim his beard and scrub while I cooked.

Possible tried to cheer me with the story of Colter's escape from the Indians. He meant to show how many dangers a man can live through, but I could only keep score of how many times Will and Les would have been killed. He gave up, ate supper in silence and rolled in his blanket.

Uncle Fritz and I dragged the harness as close to the fire as we could without roasting. Mama's baby brother never spoke much unless he gave orders or ran off one of his law-and-order sermons. He sat next to me, working and never saying a word.

Finally I couldn't stand it any longer. I burst out with, "Do you think they're all right? Will and Les, I mean."

"Who is to know? It is a free country."

I should have known better than to look to Uncle Fritz for comfort. "What's freedom got to do with Will and Les getting lost or hurt?"

"A real army would march all together. Real officers would look to the men. If one of them was to . . ." He waved a hand.

"Disappear?" I suggested.

"*Ja*, then a space there would be in the line. The officer would send someone to look. But in this dunderhead army all go as they wish, where they wish. Who is to know if anything happens to your friends?"

For once his preaching made sense. "I guess there's something to be said for marching and drilling."

Uncle Fritz looked sideways at me. "And for the guard duty also?"

"Maybe, if there's something out there to guard against."

"How do you know nothing is out there unless the guard is at his post?" He picked out a place where two strips of leather were joined. "If this breaks, the harness falls from a mule. The wagon pulls sideways. It may fall and hit other wagons. Many can be hurt or killed. Every part must be in order or all may be lost."

I sighed and picked up another set of harness. "All right, I'm working."

It wasn't till I lay in my blankets that it came to me Uncle Fritz hadn't been talking about mending harness but standing guard. I'd noticed he mostly checked harness when Possible said there'd be a strain on it. Which proved there wasn't much sense walking a guard post unless there were Indians around. And Possible would know about them. But there were other things besides Indians.

All around the camp, wolves howled and my fears for Will and Les returned, stronger than ever.

Ambush at Apache Pass

8

Wolves prowled my dreams so when Possible's caterwauling woke me, it was natural I'd think wolves had attacked the camp. Soon as my eyes blinked clear I could tell his wrastling partner was human. My first guess was Rufus Purdy, but the moonlight was too dim for making sure. Uncle Fritz hopped about barefoot, waving a thick cottonwood branch, but the fighters tumbled so he couldn't get a lick in. Before I untangled myself from the blanket, the fight was over.

"I got the sneaking varmint," Possible said.

From the gurgling, he had the prowler by the neck. Uncle Fritz tossed the branch on the glowing coals. Soon as it caught, Possible grabbed a handful of his victim's hair.

"Let's see what we got hold of." He turned the face toward the firelight, cussed and turned him loose.

Les rubbed his throat and said hoarsely, "You're like to kill me that way."

"What did you expect sneaking around here in the middle of the night, crawling over folks like a thieving Injun."

"Trouble over there?" called a sleepy voice from down the wagon line.

"Just a bad dream," I answered.

"Might as well get breakfast," Possible grumbled. "Ain't but two snores afore daylight."

"I can't stay," Les said. "I'm supposed to be on guard duty."

"Deserter!" Uncle Fritz grabbed another cottonwood branch. Les flung his arms up to shield his head.

"I had to leave my post, Mr. Fritz," he cried. "Will's sick to dying and Hank Fletcher wouldn't let me come for help."

Uncle Fritz lowered his club. "What is this?"

"Will's awful sick. That's why we were so late getting in. I thought I'd never get Will to camp. We could see the fires from way off, but it seemed like we couldn't reach them. Just kept going and going with the fires never a step closer."

"Where's Will?" I asked.

"Back there." He jerked his head toward the army camp. "I reckon I should have come straight here, but I wasn't sure how easy I could find your wagon. Besides, Will couldn't go no further. I wanted to come get you, but that stinking Lieutenant Fletcher wouldn't let me leave. Gotta stay with the troops, he said. I tell you, Quince, Will can't keep up with the troops."

"You should take your friend to the wagon for the sick," Uncle Fritz told him. "And you should not desert your post."

"There ain't any ambulance. All we got are those supply wagons and only the Lord knows where they are. We're back on half rations again." Les rubbed his eyes. "I don't rightly know if we even got doctors. The regulars must have one, but he couldn't see to all of us, that's sure."

With his wind and alkali burn, I couldn't judge Uncle Fritz's temper till he roared, "No food, no clothes, no wagons for the sick, no doctor. What kind of army is this?"

"It's a stinking army," Les said. "And the officers smell worst of all."

Another Rufus Purdy in the making, I thought, but only said, "I'll go fetch Will."

"Those stinking officers won't let you take him," Les insisted. "Hank Fletcher will say he's deserting."

Possible rose and stretched. He thrust a knife through his belt and hefted his gun. "Let's go get him, Quince. I don't aim to miss breakfast."

"Quince will cook the breakfast," said Uncle Fritz. "I will carry the boy."

Uncle Fritz's look stopped any argument I might have thought up.

"Make room for your friend in the wagon," he ordered. "And make ready the medicines."

I got everything done, including breakfast, and still had time to pace back and forth, straining eyes and ears for sign of them. I'd about decided to try finding Will on my own, when I saw them returning. Uncle Fritz marched regular as a clockwork soldier, though he carried Will in his arms. Possible followed, strolling loose and easy.

"What's the matter with him?" I asked, trying to get a glimpse of Will's face.

Uncle Fritz rumbled like an overheated riverboat, but he stalked past me without a word.

"Measles," Possible said. "Breakfast ready?"

"Been ready and burned for hours." I hurried to the wagon. Uncle Fritz was settling Will in the nest I'd fixed with bolts of calico. I couldn't see anything but a dark shape.

"Will?" I called softly.

He made an answer too weak for me to catch.

"You'll be all right now." But I wasn't so sure when Uncle Fritz wrapped all our blankets around him. "He'll suffocate in those."

"You are a doctor?" Uncle Fritz's tone riled me.

"No and neither are you."

"I am not a trader, but I drive the mules. I am not a doctor, but I do as It Is Possible tells me. Where is the medicine?"

He acted as if he expected it to be buried under Will. I handed him the paper packets and watched him dose Will with quinine.

"Go eat," he ordered. "I will watch until you finish."

"Will he be all right?"

"I am not a doctor."

Since I couldn't find a short answer fit for the ears of Mama's sweet baby brother, I took my mad out on Possible.

"Breakfast isn't fit for hog slop," I told him. "What took you so blamed long?"

He grinned. "Well, I'll tell you, hoss. Colonel Doniphan wasn't exactly expecting visitors at this hour."

"You mean Uncle Fritz woke up Colonel Doniphan?"

"Surprised me too. I figured on him making straight for General Kearny."

"Why didn't you just walk in and get Will? Why bother any of the officers?"

"You know Eins-Zwei better'n that. Everything in order is his way." Possible poured himself more coffee and blew noisily over the tin rim. "First he reported Les for leaving his post, told why, and then just so's not to waste the trip, he let Colonel Doniphan know what he thinks of the Grand Dunderhead Army. Course, I don't expect the colonel caught more'n half of it, your uncle running off into German the way he did."

I didn't know whether to laugh or rage. From the bit I'd seen and heard of Colonel Doniphan, size was all he shared with Uncle Fritz. The redheaded colonel went at everything slow and easy, never raising his voice. What had he thought of Uncle Fritz, bellowing German and waving his arms like reeds in a gale?

It didn't seem likely an even-tempered man like Colonel Doniphan would take action against us, but putting a title to a man's name did peculiar things to him. I'd heard complaints against Independence boys

112

who'd been elected to officer rank. Hank Fletcher was a prime example. It dumped another worry into my mind's fret box, which was already overstuffed.

While Uncle Fritz ate, cleaned camp and brought in the mules, I crouched in the stuffy wagon listening to Will's open-mouthed breathing. There didn't seem much I could do but pray that his chest kept rising and falling.

"How is he?" Uncle Fritz asked when I went to help him *eins-zwei*.

"Half sleeping, half out of his head."

"When the rash comes fully out, he will be better."

If he didn't dry up and blow away before then. I rode in the back all day, sweating wet and my innards jolted by the wagon. How Will could live under those blankets was beyond understanding, but Uncle Fritz wouldn't let me so much as loosen them around Will's neck. By late afternoon the fever had sweated out. When we camped, Uncle Fritz opened the blankets to check on the rash. Measles covered Will from his toes to the inside of his ears.

The day's run had been seventeen miles, all of it up the steep slopes leading to Raton Pass. By cuss and by grit the Grand Army had kept together. Campfires glowed two miles up and down the mountain.

I boiled chunks of salt pork with a few scrawny greens Possible had found on his scouting.

"Best I could do," he said as he dropped them in the coffee pot I used for a soup kettle. "Should be berries and greens in plenty, but there's been no rain in thirty days."

113

"We must have gotten it all in Missouri." We'd cussed bog holes and swampy prairie from Independence to Cottonwood Creek. Now we were in the middle of a drought. The streams were down to puddles and some of those vanished before all the stock was watered. At least the puddles spread out along the stream bed to accommodate the army and wagon trains without crowding.

While I ruminated the injustice of too much water in Missouri and not enough in New Mexico, Uncle Fritz disappeared in the direction of Stubby Bowers's wagon, a bolt of dark calico under his arm. He returned with half the bolt and two handfuls of brown rice. Pork, greens and rice made a poor soup, but I spooned two cups of it down Will's gullet and he seemed better for it. Though still a bit feverish, he drifted into a true healing sleep.

Uncle Fritz ate and rolled into his blankets. He was snoring by the time I cleaned out the pot and boiled coffee for Possible and me. We'd just finished our second cups and were thinking of turning in when Les showed up asking after Will.

"Took you long enough to remember him," I said.

"I had to wait my turn at the bucket," he told us. "I don't have fifty cents."

"What's fifty cents got to do with a bucket?" Even if he wanted to buy one, fifty cents wouldn't be enough. Not at the rates Stubby Bowers charged Uncle Fritz.

Les explained that no horses were allowed to drink at the army's shallow pools. All water for stock had to be carried, and since none of the volunteers had thought to include buckets with their gear, they had to wait hours for a turn with the regular army's few buckets or rent leather ones from the traders at fifty cents a trip.

"Stubby Bowers," I guessed.

"He's the one started it," Les admitted. "And he seems to have the most extra buckets."

"That mealy-mouthed penny pincher." Then I remembered that Les was in the infantry. "What do you need with a bucket?"

Les looked surprised. "Why, for the horses. Will's and Rufus's. And that's what I want to ask—"

"Where did you get horses?" I interrupted.

"Now, Quince, I told you Rufus would bring them back."

"Will's too?"

"Sure. Rufus is the greatest tracker in this army."

"Then how come he didn't find your horse?"

"Now, Quince, there's some things even Rufus can't do."

And returning Les's horse was one of them. His own, yes. Rufus wouldn't put himself in the infantry, especially when he could just as easy return Will's horse and keep his enemy where he could watch him. But there'd been no reason for Rufus to fetch Les's horse as well. In fact, Les in the infantry left Rufus alone with Will to work out his grudge. And why lose the sale of another horse?

For I was sure as sunrise that Rufus, in cahoots with the Mexicans, had set off that stampede and the only reason Rufus stayed with the army was to collect his share of the profits in Santa Fé. Evening his score with Will and me was just extra gravy on his taters.

At least Will's measles would keep him out of Rufus Purdy's reach. But Rufus would be out of our sight, too. So far, only Armijo knew if Rufus had other devilment planned.

While I worried, Les rambled on about how hard Rufus had tried to find his horse. From the sound of it, Les would crawl to Santa Fé if Rufus asked him to. Already Les was watering Rufus's horse. Rufus this; Rufus that . . . it made my head spin.

"So he got the horses back," I snapped.

Les shut up. The dizziness passed and I felt better.

"Feeling poorly?" Possible asked.

"It's nothing."

"That's possible. Better get some sleep though. To-morrow's likely to be somewhat strainful." He moved off to follow his own advice, then called over his shoulder, "If you don't have a bucket, Les, try using your hat."

Les pulled off his battered felt hat and looked inside the crown. "I never thought of that. It'd take twice as many trips but I wouldn't have to wait all night."

"It would take you even less time if Rufus watered his own horse," I suggested.

"Now, Quince, you know how busy Rufus is."

"No, I don't. You tell me." But the way I said it put Les's back up.

"Before I go," he said stiff as Uncle Fritz, "I want to ask you about Will's horse. I rode it today. With him sick and all, I figured he wouldn't mind." Then he stopped trying to talk dignified and asked anxiously, "Will won't mind if I ride his horse, will he, Quince?"

"Course not. Somebody's got to care for it. Best it be you." And I might sift something important from Les's endless psalms in praise of holy Rufus. If my head didn't stop spinning. I hadn't felt so queer since I'd crouched in the empty rain barrel at school and let the boys roll it around on its rim. Before Les was out of earshot, I was flat on my blankets.

I felt better next morning, which was a good thing for all of us. Will was too weak to do anything for himself and we'd never have caught up in time if Possible hadn't lent a hand. Uncle Fritz volunteered to drive while I rode in back, trying to save Will from being knocked about. Before long the dizziness came back. My ears rang, too, and they felt clogged enough to muffle sound.

Shortly after our last rest stop on the climb to Raton Pass, Uncle Fritz yelled for a cloth. I tore six inches from the half bolt of calico left from his trade for rice. A half mile later he demanded more. Before we made camp I'd handed better than two yards of calico out the front opening of the wagon. We'd passed a good many broken wagons, none of them from Cy's train, and I figured Uncle Fritz was rigging up a flag system of some kind.

Sunset caught us two miles short of the pass's summit. I heard Cy ride by ordering everyone to pull onto whatever level ground they could find and not make any try at forming a square. The wagon soon creaked to a halt. I jumped out the back and threw rocks behind the wheels. Uncle Fritz set the brake and climbed down. One look at his face scared me witless.

"Now what did you do?" I yelled at him. Dried blood smeared his face and matted his beard. His shirt front was gory as an Indian torture victim. "How the blazes did you get mule-kicked just sitting on the seat? Can't you leave anything alone?"

I'd heard tell of setting broken legs, but how did you splint a broken nose? I was so frantic and helpless that I jigged around him like I was barefoot on hot coals. Bring him back in one piece, Pa had said.

"Your teeth!" I shouted. "Did you lose any teeth?"

I jabbed a finger in his beard where I guessed his mouth to be. He pushed my hand away.

"I have lost nothing but the blood from my nose."

"You don't just get a nosebleed for no reason. What hit you?"

"There is no reason. The blood just comes." He turned away, holding his head tilted back. "I want to wash."

For once I was glad to have him take time cleaning up. Not that it did much good. Before we got the mules staked out, his nose was bleeding again. I gave him a half yard of calico and warned him to sit well back from the fire while I cooked.

Possible strolled up and peered curiously at Uncle Fritz. "Get mule-kicked?"

"*Nein!*"

"Bite yourself?"

I tried not to grin. Uncle Fritz opened his mouth to

118

answer, then quickly covered the lower part of his face with the bloody cloth.

"Nosebleed," I told Possible. "He's had it off and on all afternoon."

"Thin air," said the trapper. "It'll pass when we get down the other side."

"Could thin air make a person dizzy?"

"Your ears ringing too? That's the mountains, all right. Higher you go, the thinner the air."

"How high are we?"

"Nearly the top. I heard one of them regular officers tell Colonel Doniphan we're seven thousand feet above sea level. How does he figure that when we're seeing from off the top of the mountain?"

Uncle Fritz said something but his drip rag muffled the words.

"Maybe he means we can see seven thousand feet from here," I suggested.

"Then he'll have to change his level tomorrow," said the trapper. "You can see near a hundred miles from the pass."

He'd brought no greens, so the soup was salt pork and the last of the rice. Will ate it all and a biscuit besides. His hands shook so that I still had to feed him, but next morning he insisted on sitting with Uncle Fritz on the seat. Uncle Fritz made him settle for being propped up near the tailgate. I tied back the covering so he had a clear view to the rear. He wouldn't get much breeze, but he'd miss the worst of the dust.

Not having formed a square the night before, the wagons didn't move out in proper lines. Cy and Possible rode back and forth trying to get the train organized, but it was no use. Boulders blocked the trail and ravines ate its edges. Wagons split axles, lost wheels and overturned on the steep rocky slopes. I had to take over the driving so Uncle Fritz could help clear the trail or scout a boulder-free path around a broken wagon. It was every wagon on its own and we were soon as scattered as the army.

Groups of volunteers lounged under twisted cypress trees or took off on private hunting parties. Uncle Fritz might have sermonized them into line, but he was considerably hampered by his bleeding nose. My thin-air sickness cleared, but Uncle Fritz's nose continued to spurt off and on even after we reached the golden valley, which was drought dry and hot as a three-forge smithy in July.

With breakdowns, detours and general confusion, Cy came off the mountain with only four of his own eleven wagons, two strangers from another train and five from our own, including us. Possible led us across the valley to a waterhole, where we found the infantry being put through a half-hearted drill. Cy ordered us to pull up and wait for the rest of the wagons.

They were two days straggling in, along with the Grand Army, and some never did make it. Much as I hated to admit it, Uncle Fritz's fussing over harness and axles had gotten us through where newer, unchecked wagons had failed. But that didn't excuse him for siding with Governor Armijo.

The afternoon the German artillery from St. Louis dragged in, five Mexican spies were caught outside camp. They looked funny sitting their runty donkeys, their bare feet nearly dragging in the dust. But questioning them brought out serious news. Armijo had declared martial law and was mustering all forces in New Mexico as well as every able-bodied man in Santa Fé.

"This Governor Armijo knows how to govern," said Uncle Fritz. "First is the tax for governing the city. When all is law and order, everyone obeys when he calls. His soldiers will be well armed and when the officers command, the soldiers will obey. This is a battle with only one end."

He at least had the sense to look sorry.

Will got slowly to his feet. "I'm going to see Les about my horse."

"You're not strong enough," I told him. "You've only been on your feet two days."

"I can sit a horse just as well as a wagon seat."

"He must do what he feels," said Uncle Fritz, but he signed me to follow Will. I'd have gone anyhow.

We found Les and Rufus waiting their turns at one of the small kegs the volunteers were using for target practice. Before I had a chance to see what they could do, Colonel Doniphan rode into the group. His horse was of a size to equal the rider, but it looked worn as our mules. The colonel slouched in the saddle, whittling a gnarled root, until everyone had said howdy and finished jostling.

"From the way you boys are practicing I guess you know Governor Armijo's planning a warm reception for us." He spoke softly and I wondered if anyone behind me could hear. They must have, 'cause when he asked how many rounds of ammunition they had left, answers came from all over.

The colonel raised both hands for silence, the knife in one and the rough carving in the other. "I heard someone say five. Any of you have more than five rounds?"

Silence. He went back to his whittling, calm as if sitting by the stove in Pa's store.

"Now I'll tell you, boys, the supply wagons are still back in the pass. Until they catch up, lead and powder are in short supply. I admire your spirit, but you might better save what lead we have for Armijo's little welcoming committee."

Little! Possible had helped question the Mexican spies and repeated what he'd learned. Besides three hundred Mexican dragoons and all Santa Fé men between fifteen and fifty, Armijo was calling in two thousand Indians and twelve hundred more dragoons. Knowing how the volunteers blew rumors out of size, it was small wonder they shuffled their feet and looked anywhere but at Colonel Doniphan.

"I'll tell you something else," the colonel continued. "General Kearny's just had word that General Taylor has taken Matamoros and Camargo. General Wool is in San Antonio, ready to chase the Mexicans out of Chihuahua."

A couple volunteers got off cheers.

Colonel Doniphan raised his voice. "This is an almighty army, boys. And it's volunteers like us who are fighting and winning with General Taylor. We got the

Mexicans bumfuzzled on all sides and when we meet Armijo's bunch, we'll give them what for."

This time cheers rose from all throats. Mine, too, though I had to give half my attention to keeping Will on his feet. By the time I got him back to the wagon he admitted he'd best wait a few days to claim his horse.

We pulled out next morning, the army leading and the wagons staying close as they could. The heat drained me weak as Will, and water was scarce. All day we eyed thunderclouds and lightning to the northwest, but not a drop of rain fell near us.

The army's supply wagons were still missing and we began feeling pinched in the belly ourselves. Our rations hadn't been planned to last until mid-August. Uncle Fritz didn't help tempers any by telling us how strong law and order made Governor Armijo. When Mexican soldiers rode in with a letter for General Kearny, I suspected he might be right.

The Mexican uniforms were gayer than any Sunday dress I'd ever seen in Independence. Buckles, belts, and boots gleamed in the sunlight, and their horses were fresh and dancing. Uncle Fritz was right. What would a couple thousand like them do to the half-starved Grand Army?

We were on the move again before we heard the message in Armijo's letter. The Mexican governor wished to meet General Kearny just this side of Las Vegas, a fair-sized town two days' march from Santa Fé, to discuss the war.

"Discuss!" roared Uncle Fritz. "Wars are not discussed until they have been fought."

"It seems this one will soon be fought," Will said from between us on the wagon seat. "Troops must be waiting for us in Las Vegas if Governor Armijo asks to meet us this side of the town."

At the next rest stop he went off to find Les and rejoin the volunteer cavalry. I fretted and worried for nothing. There wasn't even a gun in the mud-hut village of Las Vegas.

General Kearny marched into the town, had the Mexicans swear allegiance to the United States, promised to pay for the corn some of the volunteers stole, and warned that any soldier who let his horse wander into the cornfields would walk the next day. Then he marched on toward Santa Fé.

We stopped in Las Vegas long enough for Uncle Fritz to dig into his shrinking purse and buy food. He wasn't the least put off by the woman who sold us the cheese and onions, but I was too embarrassed to look straight at her. Her skirt reached only halfway between knees and bare feet and her bodice . . . well, any girl in Independence would throw herself into the river rather than bare her shoulders like that.

Capturing Las Vegas raised everybody's spirits. Most everyone had managed to beg, barter, buy or otherwise add to their rations. Best of all, the thunderclouds moved our way. But even rain was different in New Mexico. It came all at once in driving sheets that drowned fires and turned every low spot into a lake or stream.

For once Uncle Fritz made no objection to sleeping in the wagon. It was the only place we could be sure of not drowning. I crowded in on top the trade goods with Uncle Fritz and Possible, soaking wet, too miserable to sleep, and worried about Will in the patched tent he now shared with only Rufus. Come morning, I learned that Rufus was the least of Will's dangers.

During the night an American living in Santa Fé had ridden into camp wearing nothing but his dripping red underwear. Ten miles ahead of us was the gateway to Santa Fé, a deep canyon called Apache Pass. If Armijo set his artillery at the head of the canyon, the Grand Army was doomed. And according to the half-dressed American, Armijo had already fortified the pass.

9

The
Capture of Santa Fé

When we came on Les sitting beside the trail, I feared Uncle Fritz would start his nose bleeding again.

"Deserter," he thundered, though Les looked to be the one deserted, sitting mournfully under a skimpy excuse for a bush. "Why are you not with the army? Your sick friend is not afraid to die."

"Now, Mr. Fritz, nobody's going to die." Les squirmed like a scolded puppy ready to wag its tail at the first kind word. "There won't be any real fighting."

"True enough," I said bitterly. "From the way Possible described Apache Pass, it's going to be a slaughter."

Les shook his head. "There won't be any fighting from the Mexican side. Armijo sent General Kearny another letter this morning. He doesn't want to fight us, but he doesn't want anyone saying he's a coward either,

He asked us to just fire a couple cannon into the pass so he can retreat with honor."

"This I do not believe," said Uncle Fritz. "It is a lie told so that you may desert with honor. *Raus*!"

He snaked the whip out over the mules. As we lurched forward Les gazed longingly at our wagon seat but didn't appear surprised at being left behind.

"We could have given him a ride," I said.

"This wagon is not for deserters."

"Not even from Armijo's army?" I wanted to ask. I didn't know whether or not to believe Les's story. Unlikely as it sounded, I'd have swallowed it without choking a few months back. Now I had to reckon with the time Les had spent heroing Rufus Purdy. By nightfall I admitted to myself that Les had lied.

All up the sides of the pass Mexican campfires twinkled among the rocks and trees. Two hundred fires and no one knew how many Mexicans crouched beside them.

"I was correct," said Uncle Fritz. But he seemed to take no pleasure in it.

The army moved out before dawn. The wagon camps were unnaturally quiet. Harness jingled, a coffee pot clattered, a man cussed softly or asked a passer-by for news. I checked and rechecked my rifle, paced our camp, drank coffee until I sloshed, and paced some more. Uncle Fritz planted himself on the wagon seat and stared up toward Apache Pass. I'd have given a pretty to know what he thought and just why he'd refused to take his rifle from the wagon.

A burst of gunfire sent me racing toward the pass.

Four or five shots, no one could swear how many, echoed through the canyon, then all was silent as before. I walked back to the wagon, so tense my neck ached. Uncle Fritz hadn't moved a finger. Maybe he'd died sitting up and considered it disorderly to fall over. I was about to test that thought when he rose and said, "A rider comes."

He climbed down to push and jostle with the rest of us. The rider cupped a hand around his mouth and called, "Move out! The pass is clear."

"What about the fighting?" asked a wagoner.

"Armijo turned tail and run last night. There's nary a Mexican twixt here and Santy Fee."

"This I do not believe," said Uncle Fritz, but no one paid him any mind.

Cy asked about the gunshots we'd heard.

The messenger grinned. "That be some of the boys skylarking. Come on now. Santy Fee's a-waitin'."

Why Armijo had pulled out of Apache Pass was beyond me. Cliffs rose two thousand feet on either side of the narrow canyon. The top of the pass had been closed with logs and brush, now torn apart to let the Grand Army ride through. A small cannon lay on its side and tracks showed where three others had been pulled away from the barricade. If the Mexicans had used those cannon along with their rifles, the Grand Army of the West would have died in the narrow pass. I felt only relief and wild joy, but Uncle Fritz pulled into himself and said not a word.

Showers came and went, leaving a thin layer of mud

that slid over a hard undersurface like inch-deep mush over slick pine boards. I walked at the head of the team to steady them, but the lead mule held me up more often than I helped him. By late afternoon the mud was dust that coated us head to foot. The weary teams needed frequent rests and when they did move, I looked for each mile to be their last. Some teamsters drove without mercy, but Uncle Fritz let our mules plod at their own speed. I fretted lest we miss the capture of Santa Fé.

We were last to reach the bare hills outside New Mexico's capital. General Kearny must have waited for the artillery. Cannon rimmed the hill, gun crews ready. An officer kept a spyglass on the town below us. Though Uncle Fritz and I stood on the wagon seat, trees hid much of Santa Fé from our view.

Sunlight glinted off roof edges in what I took to be the center of the town. Suddenly a spot of color showed there.

The officer with the spyglass called, "There's Old Glory. Salute her, boys."

The cannon boomed. Men rushed to swab and reload until thirteen volleys had been fired. I yelled myself hoarse and thumped stolid Uncle Fritz on his broad back.

By gad, we *were* an almighty people. Right here, on the eighteenth of August, we'd captured a foreign capital, the first ever taken by the States. We'd added a new territory to our country and, by gum, we might just add *all* of Mexico while we were at it. I wanted to brag on what we'd done and just waited for Uncle Fritz to give me an opening.

All he said was, "The mules have been waiting."

I swung to the ground, mad as a teased snake with a sore belly. All Uncle Fritz had done since he arrived was run us down with his sermonizing. Now that I had something to argue back with, he shut up tighter than a bank on the Fourth of July.

We rationed the last half barrel of water, but it wasn't enough. The mules stood with heads down, deep grooves between their heaving ribs. I wondered if they'd last long enough to get us into Santa Fé in the morning.

Uncle Fritz didn't look much better. Since his nosebleeds we hadn't come on enough water for him to wash his shirt or matted whiskers. The only way he'd ever rid his jacket and trousers of dust was to burn them. He dug out the clothes brush but only succeeded in spreading the dust into one even layer. If he was sprucing to meet Armijo, he was wasting his time. According to Possible, Armijo had skedaddled after his wagon train of belongings, already five days on its way to Mexico City.

When the Grand Army filed out of Santa Fé, I walked down the hill and watched the dragoons ride past. Rufus rode hunched over, looking mad as the day I put him out of Pa's wagon. The right side of his face looked blue-black, but I put that down to a trick of evening shadow. Half an hour later I spied Will and Les with the straggling infantry.

Will dragged himself along, using his rifle as a

walking stick. Whenever Les tried to help him, Will waved him away. As I moved around the hillside to them, Will's rifle stock slipped under his weight. He slumped forward as the gun fired. While I dodged stumbling volunteers, Les rolled Will face up. He didn't seem to be hurt.

"Go away," I heard him say.

Les scrambled to his feet. "I was only trying to help."

"If you can't take care of a horse, you sure won't do me any good." Will turned at the sound of my footsteps. "Hello, Quince."

"That was a fool stunt. You might have killed yourself." But I could see why he needed help to make the climb. First off, I figured his horse had thrown him and run away but I didn't want to shame him by asking outright. "You get caught in Armijo's stampede from the pass?"

Except that it was swelled shut, Will's black eye scarcely showed among the rest of the bruises on his face. His lips were cut and one corner had opened and bled over his chin. He winced as he pushed himself to a sitting position.

"I got caught in the pass," he said. "But not by Armijo."

"Rufus?" Then I hadn't imagined the bruise on Rufus's face. "From the look of him, you gave as good as you got."

"Not quite." He gasped and clutched his left side as I helped him to his feet. "Easy, Quince!"

Gently I eased his right arm over my shoulders. Les picked up Will's rifle and trailed beside us, his head bowed like our spent mules.

"How'd you come to tangle with Rufus?" I asked Will.

"Self-sacrifice, Brother Quince." His cut swollen lips blurred the words. "I have but one black eye to give for my country."

I glanced at Les and lowered my voice. "Was Rufus trying to reach Armijo the night we camped at Apache Pass?"

"I don't know. But I figured it was his only chance and kept watch on him. Just before midnight he tried to sneak past the guard."

"Now, Will, he just made a mistake about the picket line," Les said. "It could happen to anyone getting up half asleep the way Rufus did."

"That explains why I caught him bellied down behind a rock. He just dozed off until the guard walked by."

"He was sleepy," Les repeated stubbornly. "If he'd been full awake, do you think he'd have whomped a friend?"

Will looked at me and tried to force his battered mouth into a grin. "I was lucky it was one night the guard stayed awake. If they hadn't heard the ruckus and put us under camp arrest for the night, friend Rufus might have killed me."

No doubt Rufus planned as much or more for me. I tried not to look at Will's mangled face, but my eyes kept taking stock of his hurts. I wondered if I'd be able to stand up as well when my time came.

"Just the same," I said, "Armijo might not have abandoned the pass if he'd gotten word from Rufus."

"I can't for the life of me figure what Rufus could have told him that would have changed things any."

True enough, for if Armijo had sent his household goods to Mexico City five days ago, he must have planned to retreat, honor or no honor.

"Still and all, you might have saved the whole Grand Army of the West." I didn't want Will thinking his sacrifice was unappreciated.

"Grand Stinking Army," muttered Les. "We've been marched all day and given nothing to eat. We'll get more of the same for supper if those supply wagons didn't catch up."

They hadn't. I led Will and Les straight to our wagon.

Possible tended the skillets while Uncle Fritz worked over his ragged frock coat. He dropped coat and brush to help settle Will on his neatly folded blankets.

"Too soon you went back," he said. "You could not sit on your horse."

"Too late I went back." Will's glare sent Les a step backward. "That . . . that . . . dunderhead killed my horse!"

"Now, Will, I didn't do it a-purpose," Les said.

"You didn't do a thing to keep it alive."

"I cared for it like my own."

"That's what killed it."

"Now, Will . . ."

Will shouted over Les's mild protest. "No horse care

133

classes for you. Oh, no, you know all about horses. You know so blamed much about horses that if Rufus and his friends hadn't stolen yours, that poor saddle-sore beast would be dead now too."

At mention of Rufus, Les flared. "Everything that happens, you blame Rufus. How'd you like everyone downing you like that?"

"How can you take his part?" I asked.

"He's my friend, same as you and Will."

"Ha!" said Will, then winced. "Stop sharing your tent with him or taking care of his horse and see how much of a friend he is."

"Now, Will, you stop talking against Rufus. How'd you like it if I was to tell him some of the things you've been saying?"

"Go on, tell him. Go lick his boots. I notice you take care of his horse well enough. But then you don't care for it like your own. You care for it like it was the great Rufus Purdy's."

I tried to break in, to remind Will it was my fault Les had been riding the horse, but now that he'd wound himself up, he wasn't breaking off for anyone.

"After all, who am I?" he went on. "Just the fellow who helped you build a river raft and then drug you out of the Missouri when it broke up. I only went fishing with you about a hundred million years. Why bother about Will Dayton's horse? Good old Will won't mind if you ride his horse to death."

Les looked close to tears. "I'm not taking much more from you, Will."

"You already took everything I had, horse killer."

Will started to lay down with his back toward us, but as he turned, he grabbed his side with both hands as if holding pain to a bearable size.

"Let me see that." Possible strode over and hiked up Will's shirt.

His body was a patchwork quilt of red and purple bruises. Possible declared several ribs had been cracked which proved holding onto Rufus's boot that night in the alley hadn't been a fool's play. I wondered if I'd be so lucky the next time around.

While Possible bound Will's ribs with strips of calico, Les let me talk him into staying for supper. Possible had cooked every last bit of our rations in celebration. Spread five ways it wasn't much of a feast, but it revived Will enough for him to walk back to the army camp without help.

Les shuffled after him with a "Now, Will," which only brought another dressing down. When Will's voice faded in the distance, he was dragging out Les's short-comings ten years back.

From the little he said before we turned in, I gathered Uncle Fritz figured Will had been battered in a fight with Les over the dead horse. I didn't say anything to change his mind, though he seemed a bit puzzled that Les hadn't a mark on him. I couldn't tell if that raised or lowered Will's standing with him. Possible never asked questions, so I wasn't called on to explain the fight and everything that had led up to it. Only I couldn't keep from going over it in my head. It didn't make for an easy night.

Come morning, Uncle Fritz was so eager to see

135

Armijo's law-and-order city that he *eins-zwei*-ed double time. In spite of my worries, excitement took hold at the thought of seeing a foreign city. Or what had been foreign up until sunset yesterday.

Possible rode up to our wagon and asked, "Mind if I ride alongside? I been looking forward to this."

I couldn't see why. He'd been to Santa Fé half a dozen times.

As we neared the city my excitement drained away. The trees blocking our view from the hill covered nothing but a bigger, dirtier Las Vegas. Here were the same one-story hovels of mud bricks with bare yards given over to scratching chickens and thin pigs tethered by rawhide ropes tied to their hind legs.

A small river cut through the town. Canals from it watered the cornfields. In fact, Santa Fé looked to be more cornfield than city. What houses there were crowded the edges of the narrow crooked dirt streets. I wondered if I'd get the wagon to the plaza. There was no opening to turn the mules or back the wagon if the street became too narrow for us. We finally pulled into a large dirt square littered with offal.

A long mud-brick building fronted with curved arches formed one side of the plaza. Opposite was a church topped with a belfry and a cross. Its bell donged mournfully. Half a dozen dark men lounged in doorways. Nothing stirred in the plaza itself but chickens, gaunt-ribbed dogs, and half a dozen donkeys, all exploring the garbage and litter. Old Glory waved gently from a fresh-cut pole in the plaza's center.

"What is this?" Uncle Fritz stared about like a man

lost. "Why are the streets not paved? Why do animals feed here on the filth? Where are the police to direct us?"

Possible grinned. "Could be nobody paid their taxes. Or it could be the taxes went into Armijo's pocket."

"That is not why taxes are paid."

"That's possible, but it was Armijo's reason for collecting. All those taxes you were so set on paying went to keep the governor's palace." Possible pointed to the long arched building. "Armijo and his relatives lived there in style while the rest of the folks made do with nothing. Less than nothing, for most of New Mexico was up to the ears in debt to Armijo. That's Mexican law and order, Eins-Zwei."

"That's why he pulled out of Apache Pass," I said. "None of the people would fight for him."

"That's possible, but Armijo always put himself first, third, and in between. He couldn't expect help from Mexico City, so he saved his fat carcass best way he could. The government never bothered much about New Mexico, which is why Armijo run things to suit himself."

"This is worse than Independence," said Uncle Fritz.

"Most everything is," Possible answered with a straight face. Then he led us south over a narrow stone bridge to Cy's regular camping ground.

The wagons had regrouped into their original trains and ringed the town in small camps. Cy gave no orders to form a square. All his horses and mules were being put in the care of Mexican herders. For twenty cents a week we could add our team. When Cy pointed out the

137

lack of graze near Santa Fé, Uncle Fritz dug into his shrinking purse and paid Cy for two weeks. I knew better than to think getting rid of the mules would give me time to loaf and see the sights.

Not only us and our clothes but every inch of wagon, inside and out, had to be scrubbed with a soap-making root of some thorny Mexican plant, scrubbed with sand and then sloshed clean of grit. Uncle Fritz scrubbed like a boy given a special treat he hopes to make last all year. I just wanted to get it done, but it took three days, what with all the storekeepers in Santa Fé coming to inspect our goods.

With the flood of wagons that had followed the army, the merchants could set their own prices. It didn't take much dickering to discover that outside of Uncle Fritz's cuckoo clocks, our half load of oddments wasn't worth a new pail of axle grease. Uncle Fritz refused to sell anything until Captain Petry said the price was right. And Cy swore he wouldn't sell at a loss if he had to camp outside Santa Fé until spring. Independence looked half a world away.

I wrote Pa a letter explaining the situation, then spent most of a week roaming the plaza, looking for a party headed for the States. Two Englishmen just come from Chihuahua promised to deliver the letter personally in Independence.

Those first couple weeks in Santa Fé were the loneliest I'd spent since leaving Missouri. Uncle Fritz hunched over his broken cuckoo clock, quieter than ever, and refused to enter or discuss Santa Fé again.

More than once I walked the two miles to the army camp, but I didn't see Will or Les. Rufus neither, praise be.

Now that he had the entire Grand Army under his fist, General Kearny cracked down with enough law and order to win Uncle Fritz's approval, if Uncle Fritz would have stirred himself to take an interest. No soldier could leave camp without a written pass. Three roll calls—at dawn, sunset, and tattoo at eight in the evening—kept the law enforced. Neither Will nor Les had received a pass and there was no longer any loafing in camp. All companies had foot drill twice a day and the officers found camp work aplenty for them in between.

Though the supply wagons had finally caught up, meals were skimpier than ever. General Kearny had received no money from the War Office and foraging was forbidden. I saw soldiers in the plaza trading extra clothes, gear, and the buttons from their coats for cornmeal and mutton.

The volunteer company sent to guard the army horse herd ten miles out of town had received no rations at all. The officer in charge rode in to camp to demand food for his starving men, only to be arrested and court-martialed for deserting his post. I repeated this story to Uncle Fritz, figuring to show him the injustice of the sort of law and order he favored.

He only grunted and went on staring into the back of the broken clock. He didn't work on it that I could see, just sat there drawn into himself and cogitated. Something ailed Mama's baby brother, but I couldn't figure what. I ruled out measles and dysentery. That left cholera, which didn't seem likely either.

After fretting most of the afternoon, I headed for Possible's favorite cantina, two streets west of the plaza in a crooked alley leading onto the trail that climbed the Sangre de Cristo Mountains. Possible had taken me to eat at the cantina the week before, but I couldn't remember which house we'd entered. All of them looked the same, mud-brick boxes with narrow doorways centered in the front walls.

I dodged two murderous-looking Indians, then flattened against a rough brick wall to make room for a boy leading a tired burro loaded with firewood cut in the mountains.

"Cantina?" I asked the boy.

He grinned and pointed at an open door across the alley. No sign or front window marked the building as a place of business.

"Gracias." It was one of my half dozen Mexican words.

The boy laughed. He didn't look more than ten but was skinny enough to be a half-starved twelve. He rolled out a string of Mexican, pointing to the wood on his burro. I led him to the cantina door and shouted for Possible.

He stuck his head out, blinking at the sunlight. From the look of his eyes, he'd been making the cantina his home. I wondered how much help he'd be. But he translated easily enough, telling the boy to wait and I'd lead him to camp and buy his wood. Everyone had to buy firewood, there not being a respectable-sized weed growing anywhere near Santa Fe. We might as well buy it from the boy.

Possible led me into the cantina. It looked nothing like an Independence tavern, just a small bare room with a mud-brick ledge, seat high, built out from the wall. Blankets covered the wide ledge, which Possible said was used for beds as well as sitting.

The only light came from the narrow doorway and a sliver of window in the rear wall. The change in light half blinded me. I stumbled along, guided by the ledge, and sat in the corner to the right of the door. When my eyes became accustomed to the gloom, I saw Possible held a wash-basin-size bowl of bean mush.

"Hungry?" he asked. "There's more'n enough for two."

"No, thanks." My stomach hadn't quit burning from the week before. "Maybe the boy would like some."

Possible scooped the chili-seasoned beans onto two tortillas. I had a time making the boy understand they were for him, free. He hunkered down by the wall, wolfing them as if he hadn't eaten for a week. I hurried back into the cantina so as not to watch. While Possible used folded tortillas for eatable spoons, I told him of my worry over Uncle Fritz.

"It just isn't natural," I finished. "Come to think on it, he hasn't been himself since we hit Santa Fé."

"I didn't think the old hoss would take it so hard." The trapper called a Mexican word to a man in the back corner of the room. "Old Beaver Martin used to tame wild critters, little ones he could keep handy in a cage.

141

Said they were company. He was a mite strange, old Beaver was."

The stout owner brought Possible a dusty wineskin. While the trapper upended it and drank, I wondered how to get him back on the problem.

"Funny thing, hoss," he continued. "Those wild critters got to looking on a cage as their natural home. If old Beaver set them out in the wilds, they'd hunker down shivering like greenhorns caught twixt a rattler and a painted Injun. Put them back in the cage, they'd perk up spry as ever. Just depends on where a critter feels natural, I reckon."

"But what about Uncle Fritz?"

Possible squinted his bloodshot eyes. "Your thinking mechanism missfire, hoss? Your Uncle Fritz is what I been talking about."

"You sure took a long way around to tell me he hankers after law and order."

"It's more than that, Quince. It's letting a critter live where he belongs. Put an old animal in a cage and they lay down and die. They don't belong, same as the cage-raised critters don't belong in the wilds. A man's just another kind of critter. Can't dump him out of his cage or pen him in one. He'll just curl up and die inside."

"Reckon there's not much I can do for Uncle Fritz then."

"You can help him find a place he belongs. Young Fritz thought Santa Fé was the place, but it ain't." He grabbed me round the neck and shook me gently. "Don't take it so hard, Quince. Fritz is young and all of old Beaver's young critters took to the cages. If he let them go young enough, they'd soon take to the wilds again too. It's the old ones that get mortal hurt."

Like you, I wanted to say. No wonder he went on a tear soon as Fitzpatrick or his other trapping cronies hit Independence. Being holed up in Santa Fé wasn't doing him any good either. For a minute I forgot all about Uncle Fritz and his law-and-order cage.

Possible looked past my shoulder. "He looking for you, Quince?"

I turned and saw Rufus Purdy outside the cantina. He glanced over his shoulder, then stepped inside, filling the narrow doorway and blocking out the sunlight.

10

Dead Men's Journey

Stepping from the light into the dark cantina, Rufus probably wouldn't have made us out even if he'd looked straight into our corner. As it happened, he walked past without a sideways glance. Two Mexicans followed him. One had a crooked nose, the other a scar running across his cheek to a lank mustache.

"Looks like the same pair we caught at Bent's Fort," Possible muttered.

They were the spies, right enough, and Rufus seemed to know them as well as they knew the cantina owner. Since discovering the Grand Army didn't just take what it wanted the way Armijo's soldiers had, the Mexicans greeted Americans with wide grins and warm *"amigos."* But the cantina owner's welcome to Rufus went way beyond that. It appeared the cantina was as much Rufus's home ground as the back alleys of Independence. I felt a sudden kinship with old Beaver's ground squirrel.

While Rufus still had his back toward us, I slipped out the door and made tracks for the crowded plaza. I was hard put deciding if I hated myself more for running than I would have if I'd cowered like the uncaged squirrel. Quick footsteps padded behind me. I turned, ready to go down fighting, but the footsteps had sounded fast only because they were made by four hoofs. I'd forgotten the Mexican boy and his burro.

The boy's smile widened as he caught up with me. Too bad I didn't have Possible along to ask him a few questions about Rufus and his friends. I signed him to follow and turned down the street to the plaza.

A dozen or so regular dragoons, mostly officers, wandered among the Mexicans and Indians selling food, clothes and gimcracks in the plaza. Nowhere did I see a volunteer. Had Rufus finally deserted or had he alone managed a pass?

With a quick check of the narrow space between sun and hills, I led the boy down the road that passed the army camp.

"*Soldado?*" The boy pointed from me to the camp.

I shook my head, but the sentries made the same mistake.

"Better hurry or you'll miss roll call," one told me.

As we passed, the other muttered, "Danged if I'd have come back from town afore morning."

"Want to get yourself court-martialed?" his companion asked.

"If they feed you first, yes."

As we walked away from their complaints, I remembered I'd soon be eighteen. If they'd let me enlist for a half year, I could send Uncle Fritz home with Possible. Course, I'd have to write and ask Pa's consent. With a sigh I pushed the daydream aside and looked for familiar faces.

A bugle sounded and soldiers darted out from nowheres, all running in different directions. I spotted one from Independence and sprinted after him, but he lined up with the company of dragoons. After casting around the tent rows, I stumbled onto part of the infantry. The officer reading names in a weary voice had passed the D's, but Will signaled to me from the last row of the company.

While I waited for roll call to end, I searched for my young *amigo*. His worried look vanished when he saw me. He shook his head at money offered him by an officer and tugged his burro toward me. He could probably sell his load to the army for as much as fifty cents. His loyalty decided me on persuading Uncle Fritz to buy all our wood from him.

Will came up a moment later, asking, "Who's your friend?"

"Don't know. I can't ask." The hollows in Will's cheeks had deepened, and one eye was dark-shadowed, but most of Rufus's damage had mended. "How are the ribs?"

"Well enough for me to dance at the *fandango* Sunday. I have a pass coming that night. Are you going?"

It was the first I'd heard of it, but I agreed to meet him on the road outside camp.

146

"Have you heard the news?" Without waiting for an answer, he proceeded to tell it. Dispatches had come in from Fort Leavenworth, along with part of the volunteers' clothing allowance. Americans in California had imprisoned the Mexican officials and declared California a republic. It was all ours if we could get an army there double quick. General Kearny had been ordered to lead the regular companies to California soon as possible. No one knew if the volunteers would be sent back to Independence or wintered over in Santa Fé. Will thought the first more likely.

"What about you, Quince?" he asked. "What are you going to do?"

"I don't know." Long shadows and the chill air warned that dark and the supper bugle weren't far off. Quickly I asked, "Did Rufus desert? I saw him in town just a while ago."

"Was Les with him?" He frowned at my answer. "Les didn't make roll call."

"He'll be court-martialed!"

Will shook his head. "I answered for him. But if I thought he . . . Hey, Les!"

"Howdy, Quince," Les said as he joined us. "Haven't seen you in a dog's age."

I didn't waste time on greetings. "Did Rufus desert?"

"Course not." But Les's eyes wouldn't meet mine. "Whatever give you that notion?"

"I saw him in town with those Mexican spies from Bent's Fort."

"Now, Quince, you know well as I do they're not

147

Mexicans anymore. They're Americans now, same as you and me."

"Same as Rufus you mean."

Will spoke up. "But Rufus has deserted. No one I knew got a pass today. Not even for a work detail. If Quince saw Rufus in Santa Fé, then he didn't answer roll call."

"Yes, he . . ." Les flushed and stared down at his cracked boots.

"You answered for him!" Will didn't give him time to nod. "You took his place with the dragoons, knowing I wouldn't let you get caught missing role call. And all the time it was Rufus I was saving from court-martial."

"Now, Will . . ."

"Don't now Will me." He took a deep breath and calmed his voice. "Listen here. If I was in bad trouble and couldn't make roll call, I'd ask you to answer for me."

"And I'd do it," Les said.

"I know you would, but I wouldn't ask you to take the chance unless it was life or death. But if I have a friend in another company who's in trouble and he asks me to stand roll call for him, I might do it. But I'd have no right to ask you to risk court-martial for somebody you hardly know and maybe don't like."

"Now, Will, if it was your friend, I wouldn't mind helping out."

"But I do!" Will called Rufus a string of names that proved he'd been learning more than horse care in the army. "So you tell him to answer roll call for himself

148

from now on," he finished, "because I'm not risking a desertion charge on his account."

"He won't like it."

"You'll be better off if he doesn't," I said. "Rufus isn't much of a friend if he lets you do something this risky just so's he can run off to hoorah with his friends."

"He said it was business." Les's face went slack. He looked from Will to me, then turned and walked away.

"He's finally outgrowing Rufus," Will said, but he sounded more hopeful than certain.

A bugle squalled the call to supper.

Will sighed. "Time for our daily mouthful. If the good Lord ever forgives me having once joined the army, I promise never to commit the same sin again."

"Come to supper before the *fandango*," I said. "I can promise you pork and roast corn."

"If I can hold out three more days." With a grin, he hurried off.

Wood going into camp was a common sight, but I must have been the first to take wood out. The guards were too surprised to challenge us until we were half-ways across the road.

"A mistake," I called back. "We were looking for the wagon camp."

I grabbed the burro's lead rope and added my strength to the boy's. We hustled the burro down and up the low banks of the canal. The guards must have recalled the officer who'd ridden in for supplies. They didn't leave their posts to chase us.

When we reached camp my skinny *amigo* jabbered away about the wagon, the clocks (especially the broken one), and *los Americanos* until Uncle Fritz couldn't help but take notice of him. It turned out that Mama's baby brother spoke some French. Mexican was only enough like it for Uncle Fritz to pick a few words from the boy's chatter, but it was enough to get him interested. He seemed to look for the boy's visits, which came pretty often.

The next few days we burned all the wood our little *amigo* could bring us. Hail pelted us one day. Next morning we woke to find our blankets covered with snow. The sun melted it quickly, but snow the beginning of September didn't speak well of the winters in Santa Fé. With Cy threatening to stay until spring, Uncle Fritz decided we should find ourselves a house. Even I knew *casa* meant "house," so we had no trouble getting our wood boy to understand.

We followed him through the winding alleys to a place no bigger than a chicken house and not half so comfortable. The little window in the back wall had to be left uncovered so smoke from the fire in the middle of the floor could get out. Not much of it did.

A woman crouched beside the fire, a shawl over her head and shoulders protecting her from the evening cold. She looked frightened when we walked in, but after listening to the boy, she smiled and motioned us to sit down. There was no sitting ledge like in the cantina. We hunkered down on the bare floor and she offered us some of the corn cakes she was making.

"Uncle Fritz," I whispered. "This must be his grandma."

"Go get It Is Possible," he ordered.

After I'd dragged Possible out of the cantina, we found out the boy had thought we meant his house. And the old-looking woman was not his grandma but his mother. We let Possible do all the talking and then give us the story on the way back to camp.

"The youngun's grandpa died ten years back," he told us. "His pa had to have papers to give the priest. Like most, he can't write, so he paid someone to make them out. Then he had to pay tax on the papers and tax on the funeral and then the funeral itself cost some. Near as I can figure, it all run to sixty dollars or thereabouts."

The family didn't look as if they'd ever seen six dollars all at one time. "Where'd they get it?" I asked.

"Borrowed it from a *patrón*, a rancher. Then the lad's pa goes to herding sheep for the *patrón* to pay back the money. Only it costs something for his family to live so he has to borrow a little more."

"How much?" asked Uncle Fritz.

Possible shrugged. "Whatever the *patrón* wants to mark down. As I said, the boy's pa can't read. Soon the boy will work for the *patrón* and his boy and maybe his."

"They are slaves," thundered Uncle Fritz.

"That's possible, but it's the law."

Uncle Fritz looked mad enough to chew his beard, but he had the sense not to say anything.

"I hear General Kearny's going to church tomorrow," Possible added.

Which didn't make any sense to me till next morning, when Uncle Fritz roused me out for church. If he'd been slicking his clothes and beard, it didn't show. Neither of us looked fit for church, but some of the soldiers didn't appear any better.

All the army officers, regular and volunteer, had been invited and most showed up. General Kearny got one of the three seats. Everyone else knelt on the dirt floor. I couldn't hear a word for the three fiddlers squawking away on a little balcony over the front door. They played strange hymns all during the service and afterwards led everyone in a lively parade around the plaza. That's when Lieutenant Fletcher told me the volunteers were leaving to join General Wool in Chihuahua as soon as Price arrived from Missouri with some late volunteers he'd rounded up. They'd protect Santa Fé for the length of the war. When I turned around, Uncle Fritz had Colonel Doniphan backed against the church wall. From the way Uncle Fritz waved his arms, the colonel was getting a second sermon.

As I headed for them, Uncle Fritz turned and marched toward me. The colonel looked more sad than put out.

"General Kearny is changing the laws," Uncle Fritz told me. "But it does nothing for the boy and his family."

"Or the others," I said. "Possible says most everyone here is in the same fix."

152

He spent the afternoon stomping around camp and muttering about law and order. He calmed some by the time Will came to supper.

Will was a bit disappointed to find the wagon camp had already heard the volunteers were going to Chihuahua, but he had something new to add. President Polk had enlisted a volunteer army of Mormons to take General Kearney's supply train from Missouri to California.

"The Mormon leaders collected all their pay in advance," Will added. "Wish I'd been that smart."

"Didn't you get your clothing allowance last week?" I asked.

"Just ten dollars of it. That will most likely go for food. All army rations are going with the regulars to California. The volunteers get short shrift all along the line."

Uncle Fritz said nothing. He hadn't eaten much either. I asked him to join us at the *fandango,* figuring it would help him forget whatever ailed him. He shook his head.

The brisk walk to the governor's palace warmed us. The candlelit room was three times the size of the cantina, but the same blanket-covered sitting ledge ringed it. Everyone in Santa Fé and half the army appeared to have crowded in. The fiddlers scraped out the same tunes they'd played in church, which explained why I hadn't recognized any of the hymns. Possible performed something twixt an Indian war dance and a farmer stomping grasshoppers. At that, he wasn't half so wild as most of the dancers.

The laughing girls carried what I took to be nose-gays. A closer look showed the flowers were eggs on stems of rolled paper. As they whirled round the room, the girls flirted by tapping the eggs on a man's head. Instead of dripping egg, the hollow shells spilled bright snips of paper. When a girl broke an egg flower on me, I asked her mother for permission to dance.

The *señora* might not have understood my words, but she knew I was showing proper respect. I'd discovered the ladies' low blouses and short skirts weren't wicked or brazen, just foreign, like playing dance tunes in church.

I jigged, stomped, swung dark-eyed *señoritas* and a few hefty *señoras*, working up more of a sweat than I had in weeks but having the first real fun since leaving Independence. I didn't even resent knocking elbows with Rufus and his pair of spies.

While catching my wind, I noticed Les in the doorway with an elderly Mexican. The man's eyes searched the room. I figured he'd come for his daughter, but he pointed at Rufus's scar-faced companion. Les spoke to the man, who nodded and followed Les as he elbowed his way through the dancers. Nothing happened for a long moment. Then dancers closest to Rufus halted and a freeze spread out from the place where Rufus stood. The crowd muttered and edged back, then quickly pushed forward. I climbed on the sitting ledge and craned my neck.

Les faced Rufus in a small circle. He pointed at the scarred Mexican, drawing him into the argument. As the fiddles faded off in a long screech, I caught Les's shouted, ". . . lowdown stinking traitor. Every bit of it's true."

I couldn't hear Rufus answer over the confused gabbling of the people around me, but he grinned in a way that made me fear for Les. Without warning, Les's fist cracked into Rufus's jaw. Rufus flew backward. The crowd kept him from hitting the floor and helped him back to his feet.

Rufus crouched for a fight. Les lunged toward him, right arm tensed for another wallop. Rufus straightened and took the blow on his chest. He staggered back, grinning and making no attempt to defend himself. Then I saw why. Two officers burst into the circle, grabbed Les by the arms, and hauled him out of the palace.

The fiddlers started up on the same screech they'd ended with. The Mexicans took up the dancing, but for the rest of us the heart had gone out of the music. Will circled the room and I climbed down to meet him.

"Want to stay?" he asked.

"No." Half a dozen candles had already burnt out. "It's nearly over anyhow. What happened?"

He waited until we were outside to tell me. "Les saw that Mexican riding his horse. Possible told me he's a rancher from the hills who came in for the *fandango*. The rancher claimed Scarface sold him the horse. Scarface turned informer and said he'd gotten the horse from Rufus."

"That'll fix Rufus."

"Maybe. Depends on what's brought out at the court-martial."

"But if they're going to court-martial Rufus—"

"Les," Will interrupted. "It's Les they'll court-martial. He struck an officer. Rufus was elected lieutenant yesterday."

"I don't believe it. The fellows from Independence aren't that dumb."

"No, just hungry. I understand Brother Purdy has been providing food and drink for his fellow men."

"All bought with his share of the stolen horses," I said bitterly. The very thing that had opened Les's eyes had trapped him in a snare that should have caught Rufus. Perhaps it still would.

I planned on borrowing the little *amigo*'s burro to get into the army camp the next day, but the boy didn't bring our second load of wood until just before supper and I missed the court-martial. I couldn't find Will or any of the other Independence boys, but I had no trouble finding out what had happened. None of the soldiers talked of anything else.

From what I gathered, Les had been brought up in front of a jury of officers. They charged him with striking an officer, Rufus had his say, and two others backed him up. Scarface didn't appear, and when Les's turn came, he said nothing in his own defense. The officers ordered him drummed out of the service at sundown, which wasn't but a few minutes off.

I tied the burro to a tent stake and crowded in among the volunteers. They stood around a large space in front of what someone told me was the guard tent. After a short wait I saw the Independence volunteers, dragoons

156

and infantry together. They marched, two by two, into the cleared space. The two lines halted on order and faced each other, about three feet apart. After a longer wait, Les stepped from the guard tent and walked to the end of the lane. Six guards held bayonets at his back. While a regular soldier played "The Rogue's March" on a squeaky fife, the guards marched Les between the ranks of his fellow volunteers.

He carried it off with a swagger, but when he turned to march back between the frozen-faced men from Independence, his eyes blinked and his chin rose another notch. Rufus's eyes followed Les every step of the way, but everyone else stared right through him as if he was air. When he reached the guard tent, the volunteers turned and marched off. The guards sheathed their bayonets and Les was free. Dishonorably discharged.

He stood in front of the tent looking like a pup just parted from the litter. I walked over and patted his shoulder.

"Come on, Les," I said. "We'll collect your gear and go see what Uncle Fritz cooked for supper."

While Les was rolling his oddments in his blanket, Will came into the tent carrying a rifle.

"I brought your gun," he said.

Les took it without looking up.

"I'm sorry," Will said.

"Now, Will, you know I'm the lucky one. I'm out of the Grand Stinking Army." He tried to grin and gave it up. After a minute he said, "I thought he was my friend."

I couldn't bear to look at either of them. I just stood there staring at Les's pack until Will said, "I'm sorry, Les."

"Why didn't you speak up at the court-martial?" I asked.

"They wouldn't have believed me any more than I believed you and Will. And I know what the Purdys are like. Only I thought maybe Rufus, joining up and all . . ." He grabbed his pack and ducked out the tent flap. "I'm joining the first party headed for Missouri and once I get back to Independence, I ain't never going to leave it again. Never!"

He walked off toward the road. There didn't seem to be anything Will and I could say to each other, so I collected the burro and caught up with Les. He didn't say another word all the way to the wagon camp.

Uncle Fritz had the back off one of his good clocks, showing Amigo how it worked. While I unloaded the wood, Uncle Fritz paid him. From the look on the boy's face, he must have added a few extra pennies. I hated to see the boy go. It meant I had to explain why Les was with me. Then I saw how Uncle Fritz was glaring at Les and my heart sank. He already knew about the court-martial.

"Dunderhead," he roared. "You stay here and I will teach you what the army did not."

He rolled out a string of orders half a mile long. Water barrels must be filled, wheels greased, harness checked and mended, supplies traded for and stowed. And he made it plain Les was to help.

"Where are we going?" From the way he'd snapped back into himself, I figured Missouri.

"We go with Captain Petry who goes with the army to Chihuahua."

Les cleared his throat, then said, "But Colonel Doniphan won't leave for a month or six weeks."

"Until then we camp elsewhere," said Uncle Fritz. "A lower place where the cold does not stiffen the fingers."

So that's why he hadn't worked on his clock. His fingers had been too chilled for the fine work. Yet that couldn't have been all that ailed him, not the way he'd acted about Amigo's family. And the thought of fixing one little clock hardly accounted for his springy step and sudden energy.

As we prepared to move south it came to me that Uncle Fritz had missed the everyday sameness of the trail. A wagon train on the move did have a sort of order, especially with Cy Petry as captain. Teamstering had become Uncle Fritz's law-and-order cage. I had a terrifying vision of a lifetime spent *eins-zwei*-ing across alkali deserts with Mama's baby brother.

Not everyone jumped in with Cy's plan. A few decided to take a loss and get back to the comfort of the States. Les was set on going with them. He'd worked so hard getting the wagon ready, I was sure Uncle Fritz would let him join us if Les would just ask. When I brought the subject up, Les shook his head.

"I'm going back to Missouri," he said.

But the day the wagons pulled out, he looked more as

159

if he was leaving home instead of heading toward it. I tried to cheer him by saying how lucky he was. I don't think he believed it any more than I did.

I sent a letter with him, telling Pa everything that had happened and that we'd decided to follow Colonel Doniphan to Chihuahua. Cy felt the market would hold good there even after General Wool captured the city.

Most of the traders thought the easiest and safest course was to wait for the market in Santa Fé to pick up. A good number of Cy's followers swung over to this group after hearing Stubby Bowers describe the route to Chihuahua. Just the name of the trail raised my neck hairs: Dead Men's Journey.

According to Stubby, if heat and thirst didn't get us, Apaches or Navajos would. And if the Mexican army attacked Doniphan's puny force, where did that leave the traders? Dead, more than likely.

I wondered if there was any chance Les would make Independence in time for Pa to send me orders forbidding the trip. Protecting Mama's baby brother on the Dead Men's Journey was more than I'd bargained for.

11

The Voice of the Cuckoo

The Mormon wagon train pulled into Santa Fé, hooked up with General Kearny's regulars, and headed west while the traders argued Stubby Bowers's warnings against Cy's horse sense. When they finally sorted themselves into stayers and goers, most stayed. Only 315 wagons rendezvoused for Chihuahua. It cheered me considerable to see Stubby Bowers's patched and tattered wagon top among them. I figured his terror tales of Dead Men's Journey had been a shifty scheme to scare off other traders and cut down his competition in Chihuahua.

Cy led us south, aiming to hit the east bank of the Rio Grande just below Albuquerque. We forded two sandy streams on the way. Uncle Fritz hauled ropes, grunted over mired wheels, and had himself enough *eins-zwei* double teaming to make up for the weeks camped

161

outside Santa Fé. Next morning Cy dropped his familiar "Catch up" and took to using "*Eins-zwei*, boys!"

Three days of easy travel brought us to Valverde, a town the Navajo Indians had taken a dislike to and wiped out a few years back. The tumbled walls weren't fit to pen the stock, but the valley had plenty of graze and a couple big stands of cottonwoods along the river.

With rumors of Mexicans marching on us from the south and the likelihood of Indian attack from any direction, Cy ordered us into a tight square. All stock was driven into it at sundown. We stood guard over the stock during the day as well as the regular night watches, but we had enough men to make guard duty lighter for each than it usually had been on the trail.

We'd hardly settled in before a dozen volunteers turned up with six hundred sheep, the sum and total of provisions General Kearny had provided for the march to Chihuahua. That march had to wait a spell. Colonel Doniphan had been ordered on a peace-making trip through Indian country. Besides the smelly, witless sheep, the volunteers brought a request for Possible's service as a guide and treaty adviser.

The old trapper didn't turn handsprings at the prospect of tramping the high country with winter coming on. Cy wouldn't order him one way or the other. At last Possible said, "I reckon somebody's got to see those dunderheads keep their hair."

He collected his gear and rode north with the volunteers. The sheep were left for us to worry over. Our own stock wouldn't tolerate them, and we sure didn't want them penned inside the wagons at any time. Cy split us into separate guards, camp and sheep, which meant the duty came around twice as fast. He put Uncle Fritz in charge of the sheep guard. Inside a week, Mama's sweet baby brother was the most unliked man in Valverde.

Night guard always dragged out forever. I stood sheep guard half a mile off from the small doings of the camp. It was pure lonesome sitting a hillside with nothing but the gray humps of sheep and the calls of night birds for company. The first watch I was all nerved for Indians. That wore off after an hour or so, leaving me plain weary.

One minute I sat nodding over the rifle across my lap. Next thing I knew, I was sliding full length over the rocky slope. I scraped to a stop, rolled over, and let off a squall that brought two other guards on the run. A man big as an upended wagon stood over me.

"I am Indian," he said. "You are dead."

It was the first Indian I'd heard with a German accent. I sat up and rubbed my left upper arm. "What did you hit me with?"

"My hand." The one he held up looked big as a skillet in the dim moonlight. Uncle Fritz looked at the two listening guards. "While you stand here, Indians can take the sheep."

The men glanced around. "Aw, there ain't no Injuns around," said one.

"How do you know?" Uncle Fritz thundered. "Did Quince know I was here before I hit him?"

The men stared at him. They must have wondered, same as me, how anyone the size of Uncle Fritz had managed to creep up on a guard.

"You must've taken skulking lessons from Possible," I told him.

"You were sleeping," he said.

"I was not! I just closed my eyes a bit to get them used to the dark. You see better that way."

The men snickered.

"You die that way," Uncle Fritz said flatly.

I couldn't argue with that.

The men moved off, suddenly quiet. Those two never got throwed to prove they'd be dead if Uncle Fritz was an Indian, but plenty more did. Every time I hunkered down or leaned against a tree, Uncle Fritz popped up to sermonize me. If he didn't, I feared he would. It kept me jumpy as a cat in a town full of slingshots. He didn't play favorites, either. Every guard got his share of law-and-order drill. Every one of us stood the long watches without a rest of eyes or feet. But we never lost a sheep.

In mid-November an advance company of volunteers arrived. Colonel Doniphan, they reported, planned to be out of Indian country inside two weeks. He'd join us straight away for the march to Chihuahua. Meantime they'd protect us from seven hundred Mexican soldiers they had heard were marching north from El Paso.

"We'll protect ourselves," Cy told them. "You guard your consarned sheep."

The Mexican troops never showed. If General Taylor hadn't fought a couple battles out of Texas, I'd have disbelieved Mexico had an army.

Uncle Fritz had taken such a personal interest in guarding the sheep, I expected him to sermonize about

164

the volunteers sleeping or playing cards on duty. But he settled down by the wagon and worked on his clock.

December brought cold rains but they passed quickly and let the sun limber Uncle Fritz's fingers. The day finally came when he fastened the mended back, attached the weights and swung the pendulum.

The long hand jerked to twelve. The door opened. The bird popped out and sang half a cuckoo, the one note trailing off in a wheeze. I expected Uncle Fritz to boil red and spout German.

He only said, "The heat has dried the bellows so they crack. What do I use here for bellows?"

"Maybe you'll find something in Chihuahua," I suggested.

"If ever we leave." He flushed a bit on that, but I started thinking the trail had worn the worst off his temper. I found out different when the Navajos ran off the sheep.

Soon as he heard, Uncle Fritz's wind and sun burn took on a fresh glow. When word came that three of the guards had been killed while sleeping, he hit the top of his law-and-order fever. I hadn't seen him so close to apoplexy since leaving Independence. He roared off a list of dunderheads, starting with the sheep guards and running through General Kearny to whatever in German passed for the War Office. Likely he'd have gone on to congressmen and President Polk if he'd known them.

"I don't know why you're so riled," I told him. "You had nothing to do with it."

"I am riled because it is a dunderhead thing."

I commenced to get a bit riled myself. I hit back with the first thing that came to mind. "Your clock is a dunderhead thing, too. You didn't rile over that. Maybe because it was your fault."

"The crack in the bellows is no one's fault. Also, the clock can be fixed. Who will fix those three boys? They are the fault of the dunderhead army, this army with no proper order. No one keeps them on duty. No one makes them obey."

"You could have." Everything I'd been holding down for months suddenly boiled up. "You're mighty great on sermonizing about what's wrong with the army. But when you get a chance to help out and do something about it, you sit back on your teehinder and let folks get killed."

"The army is not my concern. Army order is the concern of the officers."

"Who the billy blazes do you think the officers are? They're folks like you! Maybe they're not as almighty smart on law and order, but they never let it hold them back. When they saw a job that needed doing, they stepped right up, volunteered, and did their dangedest. That's a sight more than I can say for you."

The way he glared at me, I thought best to move out of range of his heavy hands before firing my last shot. "Remember what Possible said? Somebody's got to see those dunderheads don't get themselves killed."

I stomped off without waiting to see how he took it. Wasn't five minutes before I started worrying what Pa would say, not that he was likely to hear that I'd

166

blistered Uncle Fritz's ears. I wished Possible hadn't gone off. I hated to face Uncle Fritz alone at supper. After the stock had been penned inside the wagon square, I braced myself for another go-round and returned to the wagon. Uncle Fritz dished out supper without a word.

A rider was sent upriver. He found Colonel Doniphan camped at Albuquerque and returned with the colonel's order to find more sheep and give vouchers for them. The company lieutenant took Cy as translator on the sheep-buying trip. The wagon captain stopped by our fire after supper and told us what happened.

They'd had little trouble finding a rancher and settling on a price for two hundred sheep. Since he wasn't handing over cash, the lieutenant wasn't too particular about cost, but he ran into trouble trying to pay with a voucher.

Cy explained the sheet of paper to the Mexican. "It says that the Yankee government owes you for two hundred sheep. Any government office will give you gold for it."

"When?" asked the rancher.

"Soon as the government opens an office here."

The rancher stooped and picked up a twig. Carefully he cut two notches and a cross on it, then held it out to the lieutenant.

"Tell him this says I owe him two hundred sheep," he told Cy. "I will pay him when the Yankee government opens an office here."

Which left the lieutenant a day closer to Doniphan's arrival and with no sheep.

When Cy finished the story and stopped chuckling, Uncle Fritz said, "The rancher is right not to give his sheep without payment, but the army must have food."

"I don't see how they'll get it unless they run sheep off like Indians," Cy answered. "That fellow will warn every rancher from here to El Paso. Every one of them will pull that same trick."

Cy chuckled again at the memory. Uncle Fritz studied the fire. Suddenly he stood up.

"If you will take me to the sheep men, I will get sheep for the army," he said.

"You!" I hooted. "What makes you think you can do any better, unless you buy them?"

"I cannot buy them. My money is gone."

It had taken the last of his small hoard to supply us for the journey to Chihuahua. He could trade off all our iron, needles, calico, and doodads, but since I was supposed to be a partner, Uncle Fritz wouldn't consider that lawful.

"I will get the sheep," he said again. He sounded sure of himself.

Cy shrugged. "I guess it can't do no harm to try. Be ready in the morning."

Uncle Fritz stopped my questions by rolling up in his blankets. Before breakfast he sent me out for the mules. While Cy helped me *eins-zwei* the team, Uncle Fritz brushed the dust a bit deeper into his coat and set the battered felt hat square on his head. The brim had taken to flopping over his eyes, but I thought he could have found something better than a lady's cameo pin to fasten the front brim to the crown. When he climbed to the driver's seat, I moved to join him.

He shook his head. "You have the guard."

"Not till tonight."

"We will go to many ranches. We may not be back."

He *raus*-ed the mules and left me choking on his dust. Cy, riding horseback, gave me a cheerful wave. I didn't see them for three days.

When they returned, their dust cloud sent a false alarm through camp. I pictured myself dying by every Indian torture Possible had ever described before we made out the wagon, Mexican herders, and sheep.

"Two hundred and thirty was the best we could do," Cy told me.

"But on this march your friend will eat," Uncle Fritz said.

"If it doesn't drag out too long," I added.

Just the same, I had to hand it to Uncle Fritz. It must have taken some long and heavy sermonizing to part the ranchers from any sheep at all. He hadn't traded for them. I checked the wagon first thing and the stock was all there. I'd have given a heap to know how he'd managed. Though I tried, I couldn't pry any more than a grin from Cy and a hard look from Uncle Fritz. Then I lost all curiosity in the excitement of Doniphan's arrival.

At first look we thought the colonel had enlisted every Mexican and Indian he'd run across. They turned out to be the same Missouri boys, only they'd swapped ragged clothes with curious Indians or bought bright

Mexican blankets. They looked haggard enough to have fought the whole war. And lost. Even Rufus looked done in, though Will said Lieutenant Purdy had gotten himself lost in the first Indian village and hadn't managed to find the army until it was headed back to Albuquerque.

Possible brought Uncle Fritz a rock big as his fist which he claimed to be wood turned to stone. It did somewhat resemble a section of tree branch, but I put stone wood down as another of Possible's overstretched yarns. Uncle Fritz believed him, though. He packed that rock away as if it was worth something.

Will wore a blue, green and yellow striped blanket that hung below his knees front and back. A hole in the blanket's center let his head through.

"Two American dollars," he told me, "and worth three times as much. Quincy, I never felt so cold nor walked so far since I left my cradle. We signed treaties with Utes, Zunis, Navajos, Apaches, and I don't know who else. Just name the tribe and I've been a guest in their home town."

"There's still Chihuahua," I reminded him.

Will dismissed the march with a wave of his hand. "Our campaigning's over without a battle. General Wool left San Antonio two months ago. He must have Chihuahua well pacified by now."

Colonel Doniphan couldn't have thought so. He sent Lieutenant Purdy to Santa Fé with orders for eighteen cannon and a supply train to meet him at El Paso. He put more trust in Rufus than I did; or, perhaps, as Will

170

said, he figured Rufus was bound to turn up missing anyhow.

Next morning Will left with Major Gilpin and three hundred infantry, followed a couple days later by mixed infantry and dragoons. On December 18 we set out with the sheep, the last three hundred dragoons, and Colonel Doniphan himself. On the third day's march, a ridge of steeply cliffed mountains blocked our path along the Rio Grande. The only passage south lay east of the mountains, away from the river. Dead Men's Journey, ninety miles of waterless trail.

On Possible's advice we waited for evening before moving onto the dry plain. I'd expected heat, but the wind came bitter cold. My skin felt crinkling in the dryness. Sand collected in my nose and lashes. Great flashes of light showed us the trail, but I heard no thunder.

For three days and nights we stopped only to rest the team and carefully ration the water. The only fuel was dry grass that went off like a puff of gunpowder. Dozens of Uncle Fritz's hard won sheep dropped along the trail, the meat wasted because it couldn't be cooked. We carried a couple bags of dried corn, but after the first morning I couldn't draw up enough spit to chew it.

For once the army had the best of it. The volunteers also rationed water and went hungry, but they got to sleep, huddled together for warmth, while we teamsters hauled, pushed, and cussed wagons through lakes of sand. After three days of Dead Men's Journey, Uncle Fritz tried to hearten the mules with a whip crack only to have the long lash fall limp. If Uncle Fritz's sturdy arm had failed, it was small wonder I was so weak that each jolt nearly toppled me from the seat. I was fast reaching the point where I didn't care if I did fall and get trampled.

Then a dark wavery line took tree shape and late in the afternoon we rolled into a Mexican village. Dead Men's Journey was over.

After tending the spent mules, Uncle Fritz dragged me off to the nearest stream to sluice down with icy water. My teeth started clacking before I was knee deep. I made a show of splashing my face and arms until Uncle Fritz waded by me and plunged face down in the numbing water. When he came up sputtering, I was scrambling back in my clothes. They were warmer than nothing, but that's the most I could say of them.

My trousers had worn thin enough to see through. Another week on that wagon seat and I'd have to back away from decent folk. My coat sleeves ended in tatters. The toes of my moccasins were out and I noticed a hole big as a dollar in the sole of Uncle Fritz's boot. We'd have to buy new outfits in Chihuahua. I fancied a set of buckskins for myself. While I was figuring what sort of impression they'd make on Sue Ellen Hodges, a messenger brought word that Colonel Doniphan wanted to see Uncle Fritz. I scurried off to find Will.

Every volunteer campfire roasted mutton. Smoke from the dripping fat hung over the camp like steam. When I found Will, he hadn't any more notion than I did of what Colonel Doniphan needed with Uncle Fritz. He invited me to supper and introduced his new messmates, two look-alike brothers from Saline. While we ate, the talk came round to Les and his court-martial.

I said nothing and Will only answered the twins' questions on what Les was like and did we think Les had gotten a fast shuffle. Then the Saline boys joined a card game at the next fire, giving Will and me our first chance for serious talk since the *fandango*.

"How was Les when he left?" Will asked.

"Not quite back to normal but glad to be going home," I told him. "Course, Uncle Fritz worked him pretty hard for a spell and that helped."

After a moment, I said, "I still don't see why Les didn't tell his side of the story at the court-martial. It couldn't have done any harm."

"It wouldn't have done any good either. Accusing Rufus was one thing. Proving it was impossible without Scarface, and he was probably halfway to Chihuahua before that *fandango* ended."

"I reckon so."

Will poked the fire with a stick. "But I don't think any of that mattered much to Les. He hadn't gotten over discovering the truth about Rufus, finding out Rufus had been using him all along. I just hope this doesn't keep Les from ever trusting anyone again."

Somewhere in camp men were singing. The wailing notes of "Down in Cupid's Garden" fit my thoughts too well. When a regular officer broke up the card game, I was glad of the interruption.

"You just won a buggy ride, boys. Come with me." He waved Will and me in with the group. "You, too. At the double."

Will started to explain I was a guest, but the officer strode off, glancing back to see that we followed.

"Never mind," I told Will, and trudged after the group from the other fire.

The officer led us through the village, which wasn't much of a walk, and into a walled courtyard. There was no doubt the courtyard was used as a stable even though the Mexican house opened right off it. Enough light came from the open door for us to make out a two-wheeled Mexican cart, a pair of burros, and the edge of a haystack.

"We only bought one load," said the officer, "so pack it good and pile it high."

"We gonna stuff mattresses?" asked one of the men. When the officer made no answer, he added, " 'Cause if this is for horses, let them that rides pitch their own hay."

"Most of the dragoons just came off the trail. The rest are standing guard or bringing in cattle to feed everyone, even them that walks," said the officer. "Any more questions?"

He put Will and me in the cart to stack and tromp the hay as the others pitched it in, then left. While we worked, village folk streamed through the courtyard to visit the hay owners. We could hear their laughter and the Mexican talk which sounded a near cousin to singing.

"They must be having a party on the hay money," Will said.

"The army doesn't pay with money," I told him. The hay was above the cart sides and we had trouble staying on top the narrow pile. I called down, "Isn't that enough?"

One of the twins from Saline stepped back to study the situation. There was a sudden quiet in the house, then a backwards bobwhite sang out seven times. The Mexicans laughed and shrieked, then hushed as the bird announced eight o'clock.

"What in tarnation is that?" asked a volunteer.

"A cuckoo clock," I told him.

Will turned toward me. I couldn't see his face but his voice held laughter. "I never heard Mexico was the land of cuckoo clocks."

"They're right partial to them," I said. "I reckon every sheep rancher around Valverde has one."

For I'd never thought to look inside Uncle Fritz's wooden crates. Not that I cared what he did with his blamed clocks, but it worried me that my own bit of sermonizing had taken such a strong hold on him. No telling what his sense of law and order would lead him to do. He might even join the dunderhead army, take over as sergeant of the guard. Protecting Mama's baby brother was beginning to look nigh impossible.

12
The
Battle at El Brazito

After Dead Men's Journey, the next day's travel was a pleasure jaunt. We hugged the bank of the Rio Grande for fifteen miles, then camped for the night in easy reach of wood and water. Graze for the stock wasn't so plentiful, though. The army let their horses loose to forage on their own, but Uncle Fritz insisted on picketing our team even if it meant resetting the pins during the night.

After supper Uncle Fritz settled cross-legged by the fire and carefully pried toy bellows off two blocks of wood half a finger long. I lay on my stomach watching, while Possible ran off a yarn about roping grizzly bears with a Mexican *lazo*.

"Are you sure that's possible?" I rolled over to grin at the trapper and spied Will standing in the shadows. "Come and sit. What's the matter?"

"Nothing." He settled between Uncle Fritz and me.

Possible eyed him. "You look like a pup fresh stole from the litter."

"I feel like it a little." Will looked at each of us. "You know what night this is?"

"*Ja*," said Uncle Fritz. "But I do not know your word."

Will supplied it. "Christmas."

We'd left Valverde the eighteenth. I counted off the days on my fingers. "That's right. It's Christmas Eve."

"That makes tonight an eeee-vent," said Possible. "You sure you didn't stash away a snake-bite jug, Eins-Zwei?"

"We have coffee." Uncle Fritz set another pot to boil. Possible dragged a hunk of hard brown corn sugar from his war bag, chopped bits off with his knife and passed it around.

"I recollect one Christmas I spent with the Pie-Yewts." He launched into a story about a sly medicine man turning Christmas giving into getting, which cheered us considerably. Then Will told about the fancy Christmas trees he'd seen at parties the year his folks sent him east to school. Independence's church pageant seemed poor cousin next to that.

"We always had a fancy tree on Christmas when Mama was alive," I said. "It always looked awful small and scrawny when Pa drug it in, but after she put candles and strings of berries and stars cut out of colored paper on it, why, it didn't look like the same tree at all."

Uncle Fritz spoke up. "Did you have the Christmas goose?"

"Not goose," said Will. "Wild turkey."

"Duck," I argued. "Roast duck is for Christmas."

"I'll take roast beaver tail any Christmas," said Possible. He picked up his knife. "But 'pears all any of us get is more *peloncillo*."

He hacked up the last of the Mexican sugar candy. We munched it while we finished the coffee. It was surely the strangest Christmas Eve I'd ever spent. Especially the way neither Will nor I had come right out with what lay on top our minds . . . what our folks were doing tonight in Independence. I didn't know Will's reason for holding back, but I wasn't sure I was man enough to talk about it plain out. Not without choking up. It was a little like the first months after Mama died. Maybe I'd have felt different if my first Christmas away from home wasn't spent in a land so poor the bushes couldn't grow decent-sized leaves.

The volunteers woke us with Christmas morning gunfire and marched toward El Paso singing "Yankee Doodle" and "Hail, Columbia." Leastways, the infantry started off. Most of the dragoons scattered to find their strayed horses. It had been worth breaking our sleep twice to restake the mules. We pulled out close enough behind the infantry to hear their bugler sounding holiday toots and the volunteers firing Christmas salutes to the sky.

The way the trail wound among low sandy hills, we seldom caught sight of the volunteers. It couldn't have been much past two o'clock when we found them making camp on a large level plain. As we rolled out from the sand hills, I saw that the stream next to camp

178

hairpinned off the Rio Grande, forming a little island covered with thorny bushes. The same puny-leafed bushes were scattered over the plain.

Cy halted us a ways before reaching the army camp and ordered the square formed. Uncle Fritz followed his usual order: tend the mules, square the corners in camp, take a bath. We had plenty of company at the Brazito, as Possible called the elbow of the river. Volunteers came for water and stayed to soak their feet or join Uncle Fritz in swimming. Behind us in camp, the bugler tooted the same notes over and over.

"The boys are making the best of a poor Christmas," I told Uncle Fritz.

He pulled on his long red underwear without answering. As he fastened the last button he glanced past me. What little of his face showed above the beard went pasty under the sunburn.

"*Mein Gott!*" He turned on the boys in the stream. "*Raus! Raus!*"

There was no mistaking the commanding wave of his arms. I stood up to see a cloud of dust moving down the foothills of the mountains that edged the plain. Leading the dust cloud was the long-lost Mexican army.

"Where are my boots?" yelped someone behind me.

"My gun!" shouted another volunteer. "I left my gun in camp."

"Dunderhead!" roared Uncle Fritz. With a heavy slap on the back, he sent the boy staggering up the sloping bank. The rest followed, some barefoot, some shirtless. Uncle Fritz lumbered after them in his underwear. I grabbed his clothes and raced after him.

179

All over camp soldiers yelled for their guns, their sabers, or their companies. Colonel Doniphan rode among them, calm as the night he'd asked them to stop target shooting. I couldn't hear what he said, but he left order of sorts behind him.

Uncle Fritz wasn't more than two yards ahead of me, but he had the rifles, bullet pouches, and powder out of the wagon when I reached it. Cy caught our attention, pointed, and we took positions between two wagons on the side of the square facing the armies.

I pushed the clothes into Uncle Fritz's arms. "You better put these on."

He looked down at himself in surprise. While he dressed I gaped at the Mexicans. They looked too elegant to do any fighting. Their blue trousers and bright green coats were slashed with red. The brass fronts of their tall caps flashed in the sun. The answering glint from their lances and swords sent a chill down my spine.

I figured them at well over a thousand strong with at least three pieces of artillery. Where was Rufus with Colonel Doniphan's cannon? And where were the Missouri dragoons? Only sixteen horsemen lined up behind Doniphan. The rest must be up the trail, if they weren't still looking for their horses. Worse yet, not more than four hundred volunteers had managed to assemble with their arms.

Suddenly a Mexican carrying a black flag galloped toward Colonel Doniphan. His horse reared to a stop, pawing the air. There was some talk back and forth. We didn't need to hear it to know the Mexicans were asking us to surrender. They had us so far outnumbered, they considered the war won.

A teamster crouched in the wagon to my right asked, "What's the colonel fussing with?"

"He's whittling," I said.

"Got gravel in his craw, he has. Or mebbe he don't know about that flag."

The Mexican whirled and the banner flapped to show two skulls, death white against the black.

"No quarter," said the teamster. "That means they ain't taking prisoners."

"Pa will skin me alive!"

The teamster looked at me queerly, but I had no time for him. Uncle Fritz had just muttered, "Your mother would not forgive me," or what sounded close to it. It took me so by surprise that I missed the Mexicans' first charge.

When I squinted at the battlefield, the sixteen Missouri dragoons were routing a bunch of Mexicans on the far end of the line, slashing right and left with their swords. Doniphan rode up and down the line, shouting orders. A big brass gun in the center of the Mexican line boomed. The whole army of Americans fell to the ground. Shrieking like Indians, the Mexicans charged. Just as I figured all was lost, the volunteers rose and fired point-blank into the screaming Mexican faces.

"Here they come," Cy yelled. "Hold your fire till you can make it count."

The near flank of Mexicans charged the wagons and I missed the rest of the battle. I got off one shot in our

181

first volley. After that I was mostly seeing green trousers and black boots. There's a knack to loading a gun in close quarters and I'd never had the occasion to acquire it. Every time I raised up to where I could get the ramrod in the barrel, Uncle Fritz's giant hand slapped me face down in the dirt.

It riled me so I forgot the Mexicans. I wanted nothing more than to whack Uncle Fritz on the backside with my rifle stock. Only I had to raise up for that, too.

As I lay there fuming, I saw Will and the brothers from Saline creeping from bush to bush. It didn't take a peck of brains to figure they were headed for the brass cannon. As the attackers drew back from the wagons, the three volunteers fell in behind them. I squirmed under the wagon and took after them, running fast as I could in a crouch. We stuck close to the Mexicans and got clear through what was left of their line. Blue and green uniforms scattered like a pack of scared jack rabbits. When the gun crew saw us coming, they joined their sprinting *amigos*.

"Turn it on them," Will shouted.

We tugged and hauled the copper cannon around to face the retreating Mexicans.

"Hurry up," Will ordered. "Get it loaded."

"How?" asked one of the brothers.

Will looked at me. I shook my head.

"It can't be much different from a regular gun," he decided.

While he puzzled over it, I watched the Mexicans making tracks for El Paso. Those that weren't sprawled over the battlefield. I couldn't see any ragged volunteers among the brilliant uniforms, but that didn't mean we'd come off with no losses.

"Look." I pointed up the Santa Fé trail. "There come the rest of the dragoons. The Mexicans must have seen their dust."

They kicked up enough for a thousand men, but they were too late. Every Mexican with the use of his legs had hightailed it into the foothills.

Will tugged the cannon around. "We'll fire a salute to the dragoons."

"I know you always favored Fourth of July," I said. "But aren't you forgetting something? They're on our side."

"We won't put any shot in it, just powder. One big boom to show them what they missed."

Four more volunteers had joined Will's gun crew. They voted in favor of a salute and figured a cannon should have a ramrod same as a rifle. They found a metal rod the right length, but it wouldn't clean the barrel without padding. Will turned down the offer of a shirt.

"Too big," he said. He stared down at my feet.

I backed up. "Oh, no!"

"You'll get them back," said one of the twins. "You don't leave a ramrod in the gun when you fire it."

"And we only need one," Will added.

"Then one will be black and they won't match," I said.

"They're practically wore out," Will argued.

"The beading's good as new. Besides, they're all I got from the Indians."

"Hurry up," said a volunteer. "They're getting close."

Will turned to look. I could see my refusal wasn't making me popular. I sat down and pulled off the moccasin with the biggest toe hole.

"Tell you what, Quince," Will said. "We'll let you aim the gun."

"As if that will make up for blacking my moccasin."

"It will when you see who's returned to the fold."

The moccasin was snatched from my hand. By the time I pushed my way to the gun, it had been swabbed and loaded with powder. Will stood ready with the fuse.

"How do you aim a cannon?" I asked.

"Like a rifle," Will said impatiently. "Hurry, Quince."

When I sighted along the top of the big barrel, the dragoons were so close I couldn't hardly miss if there'd been shot in the cannon. Riding in front of the line was Lieutenant Rufus Purdy. I centered the cannon on him and stepped back. Will touched fire to powder. The gun boomed smoke and reared back. Rufus yelled and clawed at his face.

"You did put shot in it." Will had made me a murderer.

"We didn't!" But he looked pale.

"Something hit him." A couple of the gun crew made a great show of inspecting the clear sky. "Where's my moccasin?"

One of the guilty volunteers cleared his throat. "I reckon we disremembered to take it out."

184

Will looked at me. We grinned, then burst into laughter. Rufus galloped up and we tried our best to look serious.

His hoarse voice was an angry croak. "Who fired that stinking cannon?"

Will and me burst into fresh peals, pounding each other weakly on the back. It was one way of working off the strain of battle and the rest of the gun crew carried on just as bad.

"You want trouble, you'll get it," Rufus promised. "Which one of you shot at an officer?"

That sobered all of us. The volunteers stirred nervously behind me. Suddenly the queerest feeling come over me, like I was two people. One part of me watched and yelled "no," while the other part did something all on its own.

I stepped up to Rufus's stirrup and said, "I aimed that cannon and it was my moccasin that hit you."

"You're running up a big score, Quince."

"Climb down and we'll settle it." The part of me watching cussed me for a fool, but I could no more hold back the words than stop breathing. "There's no rule against me beating an officer. I'm not part of your Grand Stinking Army."

If he'd made a move toward me, I might have come to my senses, but my backtalk stunned him and it went to my head. The grins on the volunteers made me downright suicidal. I borrowed what I remembered from Possible's tales of roaring mountain men.

"Come on down, Rufus." I let out a wolf howl to

185

build my courage. "I'm a bear cub raised in a she wolf's den. Rattlesnake's my only meat and hot lead's my drink. Step aside, boy! One bite and you die."

Rufus backed his horse. "You're drunk."

"Pizen drunk, Rufus, and meaner than a half-starved cougar. Step down and tangle, Rufus. I'm ready for you now." I sidled around his horse, crouched for a wrastle.

"I got no time for drunks. I got to take the colonel a message and you'd best sober up." He glared at the volunteers behind me. "All of you."

He jerked the reins and rode off toward the officers' tents. My knees melted and I sat down hard. I clenched my teeth to keep them from chattering while Will and his friends hoorahed me and thumped my back black and blue.

"Eins-Zwei couldn't have done better," Will said, though I couldn't see what Uncle Fritz had to do with it. But it did remind me I'd deserted Mama's baby brother in the middle of battle.

As I limped back to the wagons, favoring my bare foot, I noticed the sun had scarcely moved. Less than an hour had passed since the Mexican army had lined up in all its glory. Now blue-and-green-uniformed men sat moaning and clutching bloody wounds. Many didn't move at all and never would. It wasn't the sort of thing one expected on Christmas.

Hank Fletcher hailed me, then said, "Sorry, Quince. I thought you were one of the boys."

"I am, practically."

He grinned. "I saw you take the cannon. We're going to need it."

"Aren't we getting help from Santa Fé?"

"They need help themselves up there. According to Lieutenant Purdy, the Indians are killing Americans right and left. Word is the whole countryside's going to revolt."

So that's why Rufus had come back to the army. He figured he was safer here than in the middle of an Indian-Mexican uprising.

"Hey, you!" Lieutenant Fletcher waved at four volunteers carrying wood and looking as if they'd stumbled into the wrong country. "Can't you see we've been fighting? Drop that kindling and help get the wounded into camp."

"Did we lose many men?" I asked him.

"None at all. Seven got nicked but not much worse than you." He pointed to my bare foot. He estimated the Mexican wounded at 150, their dead at more than forty. Of more interest to him was their supply train. "They did right by themselves when it came to food. We'll have ourselves a Christmas after all."

Then he broke off to yell at a pair of volunteers staging a mock battle with Mexican sabers. While he ordered them back to work, I moved on. I'd have lent a hand with the wounded except that my bare foot had collected samples of every thorn grown in Mexico. Some of them could draw blood through a worn boot sole. It took more grit to pull them out of my foot than it had to charge the cannon. By the time I hobbled into camp, I looked sure enough wounded.

I crawled into the wagon and rummaged for the boots I'd left off wearing at Bent's Fort. They weren't buried as deep under the trade goods as I'd remembered. I'd also forgotten how hard and stiff leather soles were. I tugged on the boots and packed the lone moccasin in an empty clock crate. I'd no sooner climbed down than I regretted not hunting for my burnt and exploded moccasin. Possible might have repaired it for me and anything would be better than tight boots. Half a dozen steps set the soles of my feet to burning. It didn't help any to see Uncle Fritz finally wearing his own moccasins.

"Are you dressing up for Christmas?" I asked him.

"I am wearing these because you left my boots for others to take." His beard bristled like the neck hair of an angry dog. "First you forget my boots. Then you run off into the Mexican army without your rifle. You want to be killed?"

Since the rifle stood propped against the wagon, I chose to ignore the truth about forgetting it. "You're a fine one to talk about forgetting. You wouldn't have any clothes at all if it wasn't for me."

"I did not forget. It was only that I had no time for clothes. It was better to leave them together so that others would not mistake my boots for their own."

"You're full of sour apples. You were so het up you'd have forgotten your underwear if you hadn't been wearing it."

He drew himself up the way he had that first day on the boat landing. "If I did forget, I had reason."

If he forgot! He knew blamed well he had. But just admitting he might be wrong was something new for

Uncle Fritz. I figured I could at least meet him halfway.

"You remembered the most important things, though," I told him. "You got everyone out of the river and made straight for our guns. That's more than a lot of the soldiers did."

Dogged if he didn't smile! Leastways I think he did. With the beard he'd grown, it was hard to tell.

"Come," he said. "We will help."

Most of the Mexicans weren't hurt bad. They made up burial details and treated the wounds of their friends as we brought them together under guard. Uncle Fritz and I took over a litter made of blankets and poles and carried in the worst of the wounded Mexicans. Most of them moaned, a lot of them cried, and one screamed the whole time we carried him. One, an officer from the look of his uniform, died right on the litter without making a sound. And I had the back end where I could see it all. We were making our last trip from the battlefield when Possible fell into step beside me.

"Well, hoss," he said, "what's your notion of war?"

"It's a lot like hunting." Uncle Fritz turned to stare at me until I'd explained. "First time I went hunting all I could think of was getting myself some rabbits. Nobody told me till it was too late that I had to skin them."

"First time's the hardest. I recollect you've skinned more than one rabbit." He moved up beside Uncle Fritz. "I see you changed your footgear. That's right smart. Ain't nothing like moccasins once you get used to them."

"I do not plan to get used to them," said Uncle Fritz.

189

"Please yourself, but the way gear got shuffled during the excitement, I don't reckon you've much chance of tracking down your boots."

Before Uncle Fritz could argue that, Will dashed up with an invitation to share the spoils of war. Eating dead men's food didn't appeal to me. I'd have begged off except that Uncle Fritz turned contrary and decided to go. I couldn't let him prowl the army camp on his own. If he spied a pair of boots his size, no telling what would happen.

The volunteers made full use of the Mexican supplies. Sabers, silver-handled daggers, sashes, saddles, and blankets were passed out with a free hand. Every mess had its share of mutton, cornmeal, wine skins, and thin black cigars. Uncle Fritz took meat and corn bread, passed up the wine, but accepted a pocketful of cigars for Possible and Cy. He showed an unnatural interest in footgear, but I didn't worry any. There wasn't anyone in sight big enough to wear Uncle Fritz's boots.

As the evening wore on, "Yankee Doodle" gave way to the mournful "Shenandoah." I sang about the wide Missouri and dreamed of home. Then I thought of the volunteers who'd never see home again. None had been killed in battle, but more than a hundred had died along the trail or in the bitter cold of the Indian country. It didn't seem fair. The War Office should have planned things better. But then, Independence was a sight closer to Santa Fé than Washington was, and the trip hadn't been at all what I'd expected. Nothing but work, sweat, and guard duty.

Will slapped my shoulder. "Why the long face, Quince?"

"I'm just wondering if this is worth the trip."

Before he could answer, the bugle squawked off key.

"That isn't 'Shenandoah,' " Will said. "Where the blazes did I put my rifle?"

13

Private Quince aud Captain Fritz

The camp boiled over like a broken ant hill.

"Down," bellowed Uncle Fritz. "Down and away from the fire!"

"I'll get the guns," I shouted at him.

By the time I reached the wagon, Cy had the teamsters at their posts. I grabbed our guns and stumbled back toward the army camp. Uncle Fritz met me on the way.

"It was nothing." He took his rifle. "We will sleep with these tonight."

We didn't need them, though twice we were rousted out of bed by false alarms.

"They have learned to stand guard." Uncle Fritz sounded proud as the only rooster in the barnyard.

"I'm glad they waited till now to learn," I said. "Or we wouldn't have gotten any sleep this whole trip."

The prisoners slowed us down so that the next day's trip was an easy one. Then, two days after the battle of Brazito, we entered El Paso. Colonel Doniphan ordered a house-to-house search for firearms and powder. All was confiscated. He released four men who'd been jailed for months just for being Americans on their way back from California. After that, things settled down to much the same as life in Santa Fé.

Many of the Mexicans strolling the plaza bore wounds from the Brazito, but it didn't dim their welcome any. Fiddlers played in church, *fandangos* were given, and everyone was *amigo*. We traders spread our wares, though the first week I thought the wind would blow it all back to Independence. Business wasn't brisk, but we sold enough pins and looking glasses to buy fresh fruit in the plaza market. Instead of buying new outfits, Uncle Fritz and I pulled together our tatters and patched our rags.

Will went on patrol chasing Apaches for the people of El Paso and scouting for the Mexican army, said to be somewhere between us and Chihuahua. They found no trace of the enemy nor, what was worse, any word of General Wool and his American troops. No one knew where they'd gotten to, but one thing was certain: they hadn't yet reached Chihuahua.

Campfire gossip had it that Colonel Doniphan told his officers, "The devil with Taylor. We'll take Chihuahua ourselves."

Possible passed it off as army gossip, pointing out that we couldn't light for very long in El Paso. The army had to move on, and Chihuahua was a dang sight closer than Independence. Better to chance the Mexican army and tie up with troops from San Antonio or New Orleans than to try the Santa Fé Trail, now raided by Comanches, Navajos, and Apaches.

Colonel Doniphan called in all patrols and ordered an inspection of the wagon train. Whatever the volunteers could use, Doniphan bought with vouchers. Almost all of Stubby Bowers's stock turned to paper and he screamed like a mortally wounded rabbit. The merchandise stayed in the wagons, but added to them were supplies the colonel was "buying" in El Paso. We carried nothing of use to the army, but we had the most wagon space. Flour, powder, and lead arrived to be loaded on top of our merchandise.

I saw little of Will. Uncle Fritz had me checking the wagon from axle to harness hames and the volunteers were on a schedule of drill and target practice that met even Uncle Fritz's approval.

With the flood of vouchers forced on the people of El Paso, *amigo* was heard less and less. It was time we were leaving. Then, the end of January, artillery and a wagon of medical supplies arrived from Santa Fé. On February 1, Colonel Doniphan led us out of El Paso, away from the river, and onto a trail that had Dead Men's Journey beat six ways to Sunday.

The vineyards and orchards were left behind. Our only water the first few days came from stinking mineral springs. Even the mules gagged on the rotten-egg taste. Then for two days there was no water at all.

The trail softened as it led between hills of pure sand. The wagons sank. If double teams and the forced labor of the volunteers couldn't move them, they were left behind. The second day three of our mules dropped in the traces. Four wagons had been abandoned and it looked as if we'd have to do the same.

"Unload," Uncle Fritz croaked, waving at the volunteers who'd tried to push us out of the sand trap. We hauled out everything, down to the iron on the bottom. I sweated and grew dizzy because there was no water. My tongue was so swollen I made no protest when Uncle Fritz began reloading the army supplies, leaving the oddments we'd carried so far and so long strewn over the shifting base of the sand dunes.

With the wagon lightened, we pulled free and struggled on. Other traders had thrown out the army rations. Four tons of flour and dozens of mules lined the trail. The way the volunteers staggered and wove, mules wouldn't be all that would die if water wasn't soon found. Thunderclouds kept pace with us, far to the right. I prayed for winds to send them our way, but they drifted no closer. Then another mule foundered and dropped.

Uncle Fritz's cracked lips hardly moved as he ordered, "Cut it loose."

I tumbled from the wagon seat, lurched forward, and cut the much-mended harness. Without a word, soldiers plodded up and helped drag the carcass to the side of the dim trail. It took all my strength to climb back to the seat. Then, like a preacher's miracle sermon, water gushed from among the sandhills.

It was run-off from the storm we'd been watching. Water flooded the trail, swept weakened volunteers off their feet, and foamed to the wagon hubs. We dove from the seat into the muddy flood. I splashed Uncle Fritz, whooping and yelling in surprise when he splashed back and nearly drowned me. We drank, poured water over our heads with our hats, and drank some more.

Suddenly Uncle Fritz yelled, "The team!"

We kicked, beat, and dragged the mules from the harness and to high ground before they killed themselves from overdrinking. The wagon was mired, but the volunteers had a holiday helping to pull it free. Two hours later the trail was dry, but the sudden flood had given us water enough to carry us out of the dunes and into a farm village. A day's travel beyond, we found an abandoned ranch with pure warm springs. For once I didn't need urging to strip down and soak.

Will and I stretched full length in the clear water, our heads propped on the sandy rim of the spring, and watched the sunset. Will's messmates, the twins from Saline, lay on the bank.

One of them sighed noisily. "How I'd like to set down to a mess of Ma's bacon and collards."

"Maybe the lieutenant would catch you a chicken," said his brother, and both went into helpless laughter.

Will explained. "Last night Colonel Doniphan noticed a suspicious bulge under an officer's Mexican blanket. He flicked it open with his saber and out came a chicken."

"Then he tells the lieutenant to get that chicken." The look-alike brother could hardly talk for laughter. "And when Lieutenant Purdy bends over, whack! right across his hind end went Doniphan's sword."

196

"Lieutenant Purdy in the dust," said the other twin. "There was a heart-warming sight, Will."

"Sorry I missed it," he said.

" 'Next time it won't be the flat of my sword,' the colonel told him." The volunteer from Saline sighed. "I hope we reach another farm right soon. I'm living for Purdy's next temptation."

I spoke softly to Will. "More likely it's the colonel who'll tempt Rufus. He'll never forgive Doniphan."

"Rufus's hate list is getting so long it's no honor to be on it." Will stood up, shivered and reached for his clothes. "How can it be so hot all day and get so blamed cold soon as the sun goes down?"

One of the twins said, "If anyone had ever told me there was such country as this, I'd have put him down as a madman or the biggest liar in creation."

Will chuckled. "This, my friend, is the land God created on the sixth day when he hadn't much left to work with."

"If you ask me," I said, "he'd kind of lost interest by then and wasn't too particular about spreading the good scraps around. Now Missouri, that's God's favored country and I hope He takes me back there soon."

"Why, Quince! I thought you itched to see what lay over the mountains."

"I've scratched that itch till I'm sore clear through. I need a long rest in the States." I held up my trousers. "Now the patches need patches."

"Shucks," said one twin, "I'm down to my underdrawers."

They turned aside to the camp. The cook fires looked

warm and welcoming after thirty miles without them. Those flickering glows had come to mean home. I wondered if I'd ever again get used to a bed and a roof over my head.

When I reached the wagon, Uncle Fritz handed me a dirty, crumpled letter.

"How did this get here?" I asked.

"A messenger came from Santa Fé," he said.

"Must be important."

"Don't go heaping flattery on your own head," said Possible. "Weren't you he come for. He brought dispatches for Doniphan and chucked in the other mail as well. Best sit before you read that."

I looked from the trapper to Uncle Fritz. "Then the news is bad."

"There has been a massacre," said Uncle Fritz. "The governor and his family were killed in their beds."

"That's in Taos," Possible said quickly. "That Injun pueblo north of Santa Fé. All Americans there were killed. Things are going to be a mite bloody in that part of the country."

"Then it's a good thing we left." As I opened Pa's letter, I noticed Cy standing near the tailgate of our wagon. He puffed at a black cigar and showed an unnatural interest in the stars. Like three of the teamsters edging close to our fire, he was waiting for me to read the letter. I wouldn't have minded except that I was sure there were parts meant only for me.

" 'My dear son.' " I read slowly, glancing ahead to see what was coming. " 'I take pen in hand to tell you not to join Cy Petry. General Wool never reached

Chihuahua. He turned back because the country was impassable.' "

"Impossible," said Possible.

"Maybe. Pa's writing isn't the best."

"We are crossing," said Uncle Fritz.

"General Wool was coming from the other side." As Possible spoke, Cy and the teamsters moved closer. "Could be the country yonder is worse."

"We could cross," Uncle Fritz insisted.

"You tell 'em," said a teamster. "Us dunderheads don't know when to quit."

Because I couldn't tell which way Uncle Fritz would jump on that, I raised my voice and went on with the letter.

" 'It is a fool's journey.' " Here Pa forbade me to take Uncle Fritz into Mexico. Since it was a bit late for turning back, I skipped that part. " 'Everyone says the volunteers will all be killed. It has them all worked up. That is the reason they were going to tar and feather Les when he came home. They thought he deserted. Then I read your letter to everyone who come in the store. Now they are planning on hanging Rufus Purdy if he ever shows up—' "

"That is not the way!" The start of Uncle Fritz's law-and-order sermon saved me from blurting out the rest of the line which read, "so it is a good thing we got Uncle Fritz away when we did. Keep him safe in Santa Fé and away from people from the States."

I looked at Mama's baby brother, waving his arms at the teamsters, who were shouting right back at him about frontier law.

"Suppose I kill you right now," one said to Uncle Fritz. "What's going to happen to me?"

"That is for Captain Petry to decide."

"Why? He ain't no more a judge or sheriff than I am."

"He is the wagon captain. Because we must have order, we chose him." Uncle Fritz didn't sound as certain as usual.

"Suppose he lets me go?" the teamster asked.

Uncle Fritz looked at the grinning men. He knew there was only one answer . . . put Cy out of office and elect someone who would punish a murderer.

"Folks generally work things out right," Cy said.

Uncle Fritz shook his head, but if he had other arguments, he kept them to himself.

Possible spoke up. "What else does your pa say?"

"Nothing." He'd written that I shouldn't do anything that would have shamed Mama, but I wasn't going to read that out loud. "He wrote the letter more than a month ago. Chances are they think we're all dead by now."

Cy Petry leaned over Uncle Fritz. "Doniphan asked to see the leaders of the wagon train. I'd be obliged if you came along to see the colonel."

I folded the letter and tucked it deep into my pocket. "I'll walk along and see Will."

News of the Taos revolt had put a hush over the camp. Others besides me had received mail, and the loss of General Wool's support was being talked over at every mess. Will had drawn first guard, so I walked over to the officers' quarters to wait for Cy and Uncle

Fritz. Only three tents had weathered the march, but the officers still piled their saddles and gear in neat rows where the tents should have stood.

For want of something better to do, I strolled up and down taking inventory. Everything was so worn and abused it wouldn't stock the farthest trading post in the middle of a hard winter. Though it wasn't uppermost in my mind, I must have been looking for it all along. Soon as I saw the familiar battered rifle, I pulled the block of matches from my pocket and bent to examine the stock.

The sulfur flare of the match steadied and I held it close to the worn stock. Tiny marks showed where some sort of decoration had been pried off. An uneven spot was not weathered the same as the rest, as if someone had rubbed dirt on fresh wood. The match burned my fingers. I dropped it and broke another off the block.

"Hey," said a voice behind me. "What're you doing with my gun?"

The matchlight showed a strange face. I nodded to the rifle in his hand. "You already got a gun."

"That old one's a spare. After Brazito I figured two shots were better than one. Rufus give me so much to boot, I couldn't resist the trade."

"Rufus traded you this rifle? I'd like to borrow it a spell." I promised him a new rifle from stock, which would be my own, if I lost it.

He shrugged. "Reckon you can't run off anywheres. Take it, but get it back before we meet the Mexicans again."

I hightailed it back to the wagon camp. Even in the

brighter light, I couldn't be sure that one buffalo horn had been broken, but the unnaturally darkened spots were sure enough shaped like buffalo heads. I gripped the rifle till my knuckles whitened.

"I got you, Rufus Purdy," I said aloud. "I finally got you."

I turned at a noise behind me. Rufus Purdy's rifle stock was arcing at the side of my head. I rolled back, raising the old rifle in both hands. It caught the blow and the evidence splintered in my hands. Rufus's laugh rasped like dry corn shucks. I came to my feet, half blinded by tears of rage and disappointment. Without thought for the rifle he held, I dove at his knees and brought him down. Then came a spell when the best I could do was keep from getting kneed or gouged. We rolled and flailed, Rufus all steel fingers, knees, and hard boots. For one brief second I was on top with my right hand free. I chopped it down on his windpipe and bought enough time to get to my feet.

Rufus gasped and gagged, rolled on his stomach, and got his knees under him. I waited until he gained his feet. A mistake because halfway up he butted me in the stomach and knocked me into a thorn bush. The branches raked and tore my back like giant cat claws. I gave up trying to defend myself and just lashed out with feet and fists. We rolled and tumbled so far from the campfire, I could no longer see more than a dark shape. Officer's life had softened Rufus, while Uncle Fritz's *eins-zwei* had turned my back and arms hard. I began landing more blows than I took.

Overconfident, I tried for a punch that would end the

fight and left myself wide open for a boot in the stomach. When I stopped retching, Rufus was gone. The teamsters left their front line seats and half dragged me to the fire. Possible shimmered in a red blur.

"Better get cleaned up, hoss, afore Eins-Zwei gets back."

My body had turned numb so that he might have been doctoring someone else. Come morning, I'd feel different, but right then my mind was free to worry.

"I didn't lick him," I muttered.

"That's possible, but looking at it another way: Rufus run and you're still here."

I grunted and it started me heaving again. When I'd stopped, I told Possible, "Look for the broken gun. It's here somewheres."

Then I fell into a soft dark cloud that held no dreams.

I woke to a morning of pain. My shins had black lumps so sore I couldn't hobble to the wagon without Possible's help. I'd lost an upper tooth, and until Possible swore it was nothing but a black eye, I thought I'd lost half my sight as well. I couldn't see my back, but from the way it felt and the rips in my shirt, it must look as if I'd been horsewhipped. Worst was my stomach. I couldn't eat and I couldn't straighten. Possible offered to bed me down in the wagon, but riding flour sacks was like bouncing on boulders. I took my chances on the wagon seat. Possible climbed up beside me.

"How come you're driving?" I asked. "Where's Uncle Fritz?"

"Captain Fritz is *eins-zwei*-ing the troops."

"You're daft."

"Not on this I ain't. Up ahead is a little town called Sacramento. While you been settling private scores, the Mexicans built themselves a snug little earthwork fort. Last night Colonel Doniphan decided he needed more troops, and without so much as a by-your-leave, he swore us all into his Grand Army."

"Uncle Fritz, too?"

"Eins-Zwei and Cy are captains. The rest of us are poor privates."

"Were we sworn in before or after my fight with Rufus?"

Possible gawked at me. "What difference does that make?"

"Plenty. Captain Fritz takes a dim view of privates who strike officers."

The trapper said nothing, which proved he knew as well as I did that Uncle Fritz would make no exceptions for relatives.

14
Not Bad
for Dunderheads

By the end of the day I almost hoped some sneaking Mexican spy would shoot me and put me out of my misery. A grass fire sprang up and chased us full speed to a small lake. Horses and wagons drove in and out of the lake edge in an effort to soak the grass. I was sure if the fire didn't kill me, the jolting would. The volunteers started a backfire, which saved us, but we camped the rest of the night on charred ground while the land burned to the horizon.

I couldn't help wondering if the fire had been a parting gift from Rufus Purdy. No one would ever know for sure. But Possible's sharp eyes had recognized the scraps of rifle stock he'd gathered after my fight. We could at last prove Rufus had robbed Pa's store. There was no danger of me getting court-martialed, though. Rufus, his gear and two horses had disappeared the night Uncle Fritz became captain. The most we could do was pack the evidence away to show Pa.

Somehow word had spread that I'd licked Rufus Purdy and driven him out of camp. Will, among others, hoorahed my battle wounds, but I didn't take the satisfaction in it I might have once. Some of Uncle Fritz's worry over the coming battle had rubbed off on me. An earthwork fort wasn't likely to be routed as easy as the troops on the Brazito.

We marched the next days in battle order. Colonel Doniphan used Cy's four-line formation of wagons. Spaced along them were the infantry, dragoons, and artillery. With the inducted teamsters, we still mustered at few more than a thousand men. But deployed as they were, the soldiers could be massed in seconds or the wagons drawn into a fort with soldiers and cannon inside. Uncle Fritz, riding one of our last three mules, *eins-zwei*-ed two lines of the wagons. Since our wagon was all but empty, our last pair of mules had no trouble handling it.

Fifteen miles from Chihuahua we came on the fort of Sacramento. Facing our column were earthworks bristling with cannon. Lancers rode out, a blaze of red coats and shining hats with waving horsehair plumes. As they formed to meet our attack, Colonel Doniphan led his dragoons away from our column, across an arroyo and around the flank of the earthworks. Inside the crude fort, men fell over each other turning the cannon and preparing to meet an attack from the undefended rear.

Suddenly a wagon broke from our line and tore over

the slope toward the Mexican lancers. It was Stubby Bowers, deserting in the hope of saving his miserable stock of trade goods. Teamsters ran into the open, yelling and waving their fists at Stubby's wagon.

"Get back!" Uncle Fritz spurred his mule in front of the men, waving them back to the wagons.

The Mexican lancers galloped forward, past Stubby's wagon, and right for the gap he'd left in the line of wagons. Uncle Fritz's mule went wild, running one way, then another.

"Hang on! Don't get throwed," I was yelling, though Uncle Fritz couldn't have heard me.

All that saved Mama's baby brother was the artillery. They opened fire on the lancers, cutting down the red coats like clay targets and giving Uncle Fritz a chance to get the mule headed in our direction. Stubby Bowers's wagon got caught in the stampede of retreating lancers. Horses screamed and the wagon turned over. The lancers rode on to the protection of the earthworks.

Uncle Fritz tumbled off his mule and ordered two wagons moved to partly fill the space Stubby Bowers had left. Then he directed the fire on Mexicans attacking his other wagon line. I took my rifle and crawled out to see what had happened to Stubby. I'd probably be court-martialed for deserting my post, but miserly Bowers was an American.

The wheels still turned when I reached the wagon, but Stubby was dead. The fall had broken his neck. There was no blood, but I felt sick just the same. War was a lot worse than skinning rabbits.

"Watch your head," someone yelled.

I looked up in time to sidestep the cannon ball. I felt the thud through my boot soles. The Mexicans used solid shot instead of the deadly canister Doniphan had ordered. It was no trick to dodge the balls and in no time I'd joined the volunteers in a game of cannon-ball tag. When we came to our senses, we were only three hundred yards from the earthworks.

Horses galloped two howitzers to our rescue. They drew up to our ragged line and poured small shot into the Mexican fort. Then someone asked, "What are we standing out here for?" and we surged over the hard-packed wall. I fired my one shot, bringing down a Mexican waving an ax. Then I used the rifle as a club with no thought but to save myself from screaming men bent on killing me. All around me Missouri boys fired, clubbed, and stabbed, whooping and yelling for all the world as if they were on a turkey shoot.

Two thousand Mexicans leaped the walls and fled to a neighboring hill. Doniphan's cavalry rode them down, scattering them in all directions. Volunteers took off after them like wolves. I leaned over the earthworks and was sick as when Rufus kicked me in the belly. When I got back to the wagon, my knees and hands shook, mostly because I'd just realized how close I'd come to getting killed.

"Dunderheads," said Uncle Fritz. "If they had stayed to fight, they would have won."

"They came close to it when Stubby Bowers left that hole in our line," Cy said. He clapped Uncle Fritz on the back. "But we *eins-zwei*-ed them."

208

For the first time since I'd known him, Uncle Fritz grinned.

Will rode past on a captured Mexican horse. "We dunderheads sure can fight," he called.

"*Ja*, if someone shows you how," Uncle Fritz answered, but he sounded almost as if he was joshing.

It was well after dark before the last of the volunteers straggled back into camp and a tally of losses could be made. Eight of the Grand Army had been wounded. One of them died that night. Outside of greedy Stubby Bowers, he was the only American casualty. Over three hundred Mexicans had died and as many were wounded.

The next day, March 1, we marched into the biggest city in northern Mexico, a band of ragged scarecrows singing "Yankee Doodle" at the top of our lungs.

While the Grand Army took a two-month holiday with bullfights, cockfights, *fandangos*, and the company of *señoritas*, Uncle Fritz and I scrabbled to keep alive. The pair of Mackinaw blankets we'd carried between the layers of osnaburg wagon covering were our only trade goods. They brought enough to feed us, but our clothes were falling away to the point of indecency.

Colonel Doniphan at last made contact with General Wool. He had joined General Taylor at Buena Vista, where they'd engaged and defeated Mexico's great general and president, Santa Anna, in a two-day battle. It had been a near thing, a victory only because Santa Anna had been unable to call on the troops digging in to meet the Grand Army at Sacramento. The three-thousand-mile march hadn't been wasted.

After the news had been celebrated with fireworks and *fandangos*, Cy called a conference of the teamsters.

"Colonel Doniphan is marching the boys to Buena Vista," he told us. "He's released us to do as we please. We can stay here or go back to Santa Fé."

I groaned at the thought of repeating the journey. That's what most all the traders decided on. Some planned to wait for winter before leaving. Others said they'd pull out in a day or two.

When most had drifted away from Cy's fire, Uncle Fritz asked, "What will you do, Captain Petry?"

"I'd like to tag along with Doniphan, but I got my wagons to think of. I'll go back to Santa Fé in the fall."

"Quince will go with you."

"What are you going to do?" I asked him.

"The army still has no wagons for the sick. I will go with them and help."

"So will I."

He looked as if he'd give me an argument, but after a moment, he nodded. "We will both go."

"Possible?" Cy turned to the trapper. "I'll pay you off as of now and you can do as you please."

"I'd surely love to watch Eins-Zwei meet up with General Wool, but it come to me you're going to need a scout on this trip. Injuns are getting feisty along the trail."

So we took our farewells from Cy and Possible and followed the dunderhead army southeast. We weren't long discovering why General Wool had turned back, but his troops weren't the Missouri volunteers. Uncle

210

Fritz *eins-zwei*-ed the stragglers, nursed the sick in the rickety wagon, and took to sneaking up on the guards to show them how easy Apaches could send them under. Unlike the teamsters who'd stood sheep guard for him, the volunteers took it in good humor and *eins-zwei* became a camp word.

When we dragged into Buena Vista, the volunteers drew full rations for the first time in their year of service. Uncle Fritz bullied them into trimming their hair and scrubbing, though most claimed they had no clothes left to wash. Half were down to their underwear and some had only loincloths. Uncle Fritz stomped off to General Taylor's camp and returned with a red face and enough army greatcoats to cover the most indecent.

Uncle Fritz could have used one himself. His hat brim had torn half off the crown and flopped over one shoulder. His frock coat had long ago been discarded, along with his shirt. His trousers were so patched I couldn't honestly say they were the same ones he'd started out with, and his moccasins were nothing but soles held on with straps. I was down to holey underwear and patched trousers that ended in tatters at the knee.

General Taylor's face was a study when he reviewed the rough, ragged line. Just the same, he made us a speech, calling us heroes and telling us how we'd turned Buena Vista into an American victory. When he mentioned the three and a half thousand miles we'd come, Will muttered, "With no help from you or the War Office." Uncle Fritz glared at him. When the general asked them to enlist for another year, running off the pay and benefits, hoots and hollers came from all along the line.

"We heard that at Fort Leavenworth," one called.

"Pay what you owe us and we'll consider," said another.

"Just send me home," brought a chorus of agreement.

While we waited for boats to take us to New Orleans, we saw and heard things that General Kearny and Colonel Doniphan would never have permitted. For the first time the Mexicans cowered before us, hate in their eyes. No fiddlers paraded around the plaza. No *fandangos* were given for the men under Wool and Taylor.

"There's something to be said for law and order," I told Uncle Fritz.

He nodded. "But I have found there are many kinds of law. Not all of them are good."

I knew he was thinking of the way Armijo had run Santa Fé. "Still, not everyone can do as he wishes. Look at Rufus Purdy and the way Stubby Bowers nearly let the Mexicans through our lines."

"Captain Petry has said people generally work things out the right way. Perhaps that is the answer. But can everyone be right? I do not know, Quincy."

"I reckon Mama was right after all. You could have been a sweet little boy."

But I'd pushed too far. His face darkened. I backed a few steps, mumbled something about seeing Will, and left.

212

Next day I saw a boy not much older than our wood-selling *amigo* in Santa Fé shot as a spy. After that it was a relief to board the stinking, wallowing transport boats. Our wagon, along with the volunteers' horses and saddles, was left behind. General Taylor had promised to have them shipped overland, but we knew we'd never see our gear again.

"One enlistment is all a man can afford," Will said.

"Our partnership didn't do too well either." I opened the bundle Uncle Fritz and I had salvaged. "Our rifles, one worn moccasin, a piece of rock said to be wood, and the evidence against Rufus Purdy."

Uncle Fritz said something, but it was drowned by cannon fire. We crowded to the rail. The wharves of New Orleans were crowded with people waving flags and cheering. More cannon saluted us than we'd heard in Sacramento.

"By gad," Will shouted. "We are an all mighty army."

"A dunderhead army," said Uncle Fritz. "Who but dunderheads would have tried such a march."

"Or run to fight a battle in his underwear," I reminded him.

"Or shot an officer with a grand stinking moccasin," added Will.

We yelled remembrances, all three together, thumped backs, laughed, cried, and acted the fools till our boat nosed into the dock and the welcoming crowd pushed aboard. They lifted the volunteers, Uncle Fritz and me included, onto their shoulders and paraded us through the streets. The city fed us, bedded us down in

213

the finest hotel, and bought us all new clothes.

Uncle Fritz wouldn't wear them. "If I am a dunder-head in a dunderhead army, then I wear the uniform."

"He's right," Will said. "These are rags to be proud of."

Some of the other companies took the new clothes, but those from Saline and Independence and a few other towns voted to wear their rags all the way home.

Our welcome in New Orleans paled considerably after we reached Independence. The Fourth of July bunting hung over the dock and decorated the buggies, carriages and wagons that were waiting to parade us into town. All along the road people joined the cheering crowd behind us. Will's father had thrown open the dining rooms of the Independence House. We were toasted, dined and speechified for three days running. By then I felt I never wanted to see another piece of dried-apple pie or hear another senator as long as I lived. How Uncle Fritz could walk from the last dinner looking as soldierly and neat as he had at the first, I'll never know. Except for our fresh clothes, the rest of us looked as if we'd just finished a long march on the alkali trail.

Then it was back to work. The summer of '47 was bigger than '46 had been. Emigrants for Oregon and California argued and dickered in the muddy streets. All forges pounded day and night. Will was so busy helping his pa run the Independence House that Sue Ellen Hodges up and married Les, who'd had a head start courting her. Pa sold barrels and cases fast as Uncle Fritz and I could haul them from the landing.

Fall emptied the town. Winter closed the river and just before Christmas, Cy and the traders from Chihuahua arrived and settled down by the stoves to swap tales. Possible had met trapping cronies in Santa Fé who'd told him Rufus Purdy was scalp hunting, collecting the bounty the Mexican government had put on Apache scalps.

"Rufus stuck his head in the wrong bee tree this time," Possible said. "I surely wouldn't want Apaches taking an unfriendly interest in me."

"Long as he doesn't show up here," Pa said.

"Maybe he will go to California," Uncle Fritz said.

No matter which part of the Grand Army's march the stovesiders relived, Uncle Fritz always dragged the talk around to California. Some emigrants had told him about a Mr. Sutter who was building his own little country of New Helvetia in California. Everything was to be run as exact as the innards in one of Uncle Fritz's clocks. I didn't mind it in the store, but I'd started reading for the law and it bothered me when Pa, Uncle Fritz and Possible brought the talk home.

One night while I was puzzling over a legal problem, I heard Pa say, "The wagons are what's holding me back. Now if we could work a deal with Cy, driving his wagons in part payment, we might manage."

"It's possible, seeing as how the big profits in the Santa Fé trade are gone now." Possible rubbed his chin. "I don't know how Cy would like California, though."

"It stands to reason all those folks need supplies. Most of them will be shipped around the Horn, but there'll be plenty of freighting between towns."

"If Cy does not go," said Uncle Fritz, "we will buy our own wagons somehow."

I sat up and closed the law book. "Pa, you aren't really going to California?"

"I'll tell you, Quince, I've developed a bit of an itch. Or maybe it's just the case I had when I came to Missouri breaking out again. Besides, Fritz is bound to go and someone has to look after him."

I looked at Uncle Fritz. His neat, trimmed beard twitched. Possible grinned.

"What about me? I just started studying for the law."

"Law will be needed in California," said Uncle Fritz.

"And it's a long trip," Pa added. "You'll have so much time to study on the trail, you should have all those books read before we reach the Rockies."

Uncle Fritz's beard trembled. We burst out laughing at the same time. Possible whooped and pounded the table. Pa stood there, not knowing why we were laughing. But he'd find out, long before we reached the Rockies.